"That tub is a little small for both of us, don't you think?" Chantelle asked.

Tristan tugged his T-shirt from his jeans and pulled it up over his head. She was treated to an awe-inspiring display of abs and pecs.

"I was hoping you'd ask me to join you," he said. Tristan stepped close and put his hands on her shoulders. "If you're not comfortable with this," he said, indicating the tub filled with steaming water, "then we won't even try it. I'll admit, I was trying to think of some way to connect intimately with you. This seemed like a good idea." He shrugged. "Hell, I'm a guy. Anything that involves me naked with a beautiful woman seems like a damn good idea."

She laughed, rising on her toes to press her mouth to his. She let the heat, the sensation flowing through her take control, and she curved her body into his, her center rubbing against the hard bulge in his jeans.

"But will it be hard for you, bathing me?"

He pulled her tightly against him and said, "Honey, this can't get much harder...."

Blaze™

Dear Reader,

I can't even describe how exciting it has been to write this Blaze miniseries, The Sixth Sense, about six cousins in their twenties who are called upon to help ghosts that need a little assistance finding the light.

The number of e-mails I've received asking for Tristan's story has been quite shocking (who doesn't love a sexy fireman?). Well, here it is, and as many of you may have guessed, Tristan finds himself with Chantelle Bedeau, the sister of the ghost in *Ghosts and Roses*. You may recall the sparks between headstrong Chantelle and her equally headstrong fireman. But Chantelle surprises Tristan this time when she asks him to sleep with her, then takes off, only to return with an angry ghost at her heels.

I hope you enjoy Tristan's story. Stay tuned for Jenee's story (*Bed on Arrival*) in July and Nanette's story (*Live and Yearn*) in September.

Please visit my Web site, www.kelleystjohn.com, to enter to win a fabulous New Orleans vacation giveaway, learn the latest news about my recent and upcoming releases, and drop me a line. I love hearing from readers!

Happy reading,

Kelley St. John

FIRE IN THE BLOOD
Kelley St. John

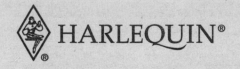
HARLEQUIN®

TORONTO • NEW YORK • LONDON
AMSTERDAM • PARIS • SYDNEY • HAMBURG
STOCKHOLM • ATHENS • TOKYO • MILAN • MADRID
PRAGUE • WARSAW • BUDAPEST • AUCKLAND

ISBN-13: 978-0-373-79401-0
ISBN-10:   0-373-79401-0

FIRE IN THE BLOOD

ABOUT THE AUTHOR

Kelley St. John's previous experience as a senior writer at NASA fueled her interest in writing action-packed suspense, although she also enjoys penning steamy romances and quirky women's fiction. Since 2000, St. John has obtained over fifty writing awards, including the National Readers' Choice Award, and was elected to the Board of Directors for Romance Writers of America. Visit her Web site, www.kelleystjohn.com, for the latest news about recent and upcoming releases and to register for fabulous vacation giveaways!

Books by Kelley St. John
HARLEQUIN BLAZE
325—KISS AND DWELL
337—GHOSTS AND ROSES
349—SHIVER AND SPICE

For Herbert and Christie.
Geaux Tigers!

Introduction

WINDING ALONG the Mississippi River and joining New Orleans to Baton Rouge, Louisiana's notable River Road showcases more than seventy miles of pillared plantations, sugarcane fields and lush bayou scenery. Naturally, each River Road estate has a story to tell; however, one plantation's story surpasses all others, because many of the individuals who visit the Vicknair plantation are no longer breathing.

Since they first moved to St. Charles parish nearly two hundred years ago, each generation of the Vicknair family has aided those of the dead who have had difficulties crossing over, helping them deal with what's holding them to the world of the living, so they can find their way through to the other side.

The newest generation understands their duty to continue the family tradition *and* protect the family secret. The youngest Vicknairs, now predominantly in their twenties, are helping spirits on a regular basis and perfecting their talent with every crossing.

Nanette, Tristan, Gage, Monique, Dax and Jenee, the six cousins currently performing Vicknair medium duty, realize that when a lavender-tinted envelope materializes on the infamous tea service in the plantation's

sitting room, they're expected to drop everything to
help a spirit. Their grandmother, Adeline Vicknair, may
be on the other side, but she wants her assignments
handled in a timely manner.

Thankfully, her grandchildren know to heed her call.
They understand the simple rules associated with
helping spirits, rules that have been handed down from
generation to generation.

*A medium must heed a spirit's call and handle a
spirit's needs in a timely manner. Failure to do so will
result in unfavorable—if not painful—repercussions.*

*Once a spirit is assigned to a medium, the two are emotionally bonded until the spirit's requirement for crossing
over has been fulfilled. This bond should never be abused
nor taken for granted in any way, shape or form.*

*Spirits are physically incapable of lying to mediums;
likewise, a medium should never lie to a spirit.*

A medium may not touch a spirit. Period.

Firefighter Tristan Vicknair, at twenty-nine the oldest
male of the lot, has had no trouble helping his assigned
specters find their way to the light. However, ever since
one ghost arrived at the plantation with her stunning
sister—a woman whose strong will and stubborn streak
rivals his own, and whose sensuality is hotter than any
fire he's ever encountered on the job—Tristan has had
a monumental problem of the living persuasion.

Chantelle Bedeau.

Prologue

TRISTAN VICKNAIR LIFTED his glass of champagne to toast the bride and groom, along with all the other guests assembled beneath the vast white tent on the Vicknair plantation.

Who'd have thought that the youngest male of the bunch would tie the knot first? But Tristan couldn't deny that Dax Vicknair was besotted with his new bride, and Celeste Beauchamp Vicknair appeared equally mesmerized with her new husband. And there was no doubt the powers that be agreed with the match, since Celeste had been on her way to permanent residency on the other side when Dax halted her progress.

Doing his part as groomsman, Tristan then visited with the majority of the wedding guests during the reception; however, the one he wanted to talk to more than any other stayed conspicuously away from him. As a matter of fact, Chantelle Bedeau hadn't so much as glanced at him throughout the entire event.

The sister of a ghost that Tristan's cousin Gage had helped a couple of months ago, Chantelle had haunted Tristan's nights more than any of his assigned specters; he simply couldn't get her off his mind. Since Lillian Bedeau's killer also had a vendetta against Chantelle,

Gage had moved her into the plantation house until they'd stopped the madman. Tristan had felt an immediate attraction to the blue-eyed strong-willed blonde, but he'd never acted on it. It wasn't the time. She'd just lost her sister and was being stalked by her murderer. But during that period, he'd grown closer to the intriguing, yet stubborn female.

And if they were still on speaking terms now, Tristan would see if she was ready to move beyond talking. But her stay at the Vicknair plantation hadn't exactly ended under the best of circumstances. Chantelle had been so determined to help catch Lillian's killer that she'd actually planned to use herself as bait in order to trap him. Tristan had let her know in no uncertain terms that there was no way in hell he'd let her put her life in danger.

She hadn't appreciated his order, but Tristan hadn't budged. He wasn't about to let her get hurt.

That was the last time she'd spoken to him.

Obviously the woman carried a grudge, but if he had it to do over again, he'd do the same thing. He was glad he'd kept her from joining her sister in the land of the non-breathing, and the police *had* caught the killer, A. D. Romero, with Gage's help, so everything had ended up the way she wanted, right?

Tristan took another sip of champagne and watched her chat with Gage's fiancée, Kayla. Determined that he wouldn't make a fool of himself by staring a hole through Chantelle all night, he looked away from them and focused on his new sister-in-law and her family, currently having a photo taken beside the plantation house—but he kept his hearing tuned in to Chantelle's voice and was rewarded when he heard her throaty laugh. He'd never heard her laugh before—there hadn't been much occasion for laughter during her brief stay at the plantation—and he found the sound exhilarating. Like the woman.

He'd been drawn to her for many reasons—her determination to make Lillian's murderer pay, her protectiveness toward Kayla when Romero nearly took her life, as well, and her astounding ability to overcome her past. She'd been raised in the same orphanage as his cousin's fiancée and, like Kayla, had been a victim of sexual abuse from both A. D. Romero and his father during her teen years. Nevertheless, she was headstrong and resolute, and apparently afraid of nothing, not even a killer.

Perhaps it was that determination that had caused her to constantly remain in the back of Tristan's mind, or perhaps it was the way she stood her ground with him on nearly every occasion they'd had a differing opinion during her stay at the plantation. But for whatever reason, he'd been looking forward to the day when he'd see her and talk to her again, and now that it was here...

He wasn't doing either.

Hell, what was he waiting for? She was here, and he wanted to be with her. And staying away from her wasn't going to make it happen.

Tristan turned to walk toward the spot where she was talking to Kayla—and saw that they were no longer there. Then he scanned the area beneath the tent, but didn't see even a hint of her.

A tap on his shoulder took his attention away from his examination of the reception area. He turned, and saw that he had no need to continue his search; Chantelle was standing beside him.

"Tristan."

When she was at the plantation, she'd kept her long blond waves hanging well past her shoulders, but now her hair was piled on top of her head in golden curls, with two long tendrils grazing sexy shoulders. If possible, her eyes were even bluer than he remembered, an icy shade that matched her shimmering gown. Her mouth also shimmered with some kind of pale-pink gloss. Tristan focused on the eyes, the mouth, the hair; the exceptional woman before him.

"Tristan," she repeated, and he realized he'd yet to speak.

"Chantelle," he said, his voice a little deeper than normal. Hell, he was never nervous around women. He was never nervous, period. His position as fire chief demanded a calm, cool mind-set at all times, which typically carried over beyond his profession. But then again, Chantelle Bedeau didn't fall into the *typical* category. She was extraordinary, and merely standing near her was making him hard. "It's good to see you." He concentrated on seeing her as she was right now, wearing a blue gown at his cousin's wedding reception, instead of the way he often saw her in his dreams, wearing nothing at all—and in his bed.

Tristan swallowed, his dick twitched, and he gave up the fight. In his mind, she was naked, and she was…his.

CHANTELLE HAD BEEN garnering the courage to do this ever since she'd received the invitation to the wedding, but when push came to shove and she'd seen Tristan Vicknair standing with all of the groomsmen, those green eyes drawing her in and that undeniably alpha male presence eclipsing every other man around, she'd frozen. Hadn't even been able to say hello, much less ask him for what she needed.

But she would. She had to.

"Good to see you, too," she said, then she bit her lower lip, decided that she would do this, no matter what, and repeated, "Tristan?"

"Yes?" Something over her shoulder caught his attention, and he nodded. "Dax and Celeste are waving at us."

Chantelle turned, smiled at the bride and groom, then turned back to him. "Can I ask you something?"

"Sure." He seemed to look at her then, really look at her, and the power of those green eyes sent a sensual shiver through her.

Chantelle couldn't deny the attraction between them, an attraction she honestly had never experienced with any other man. During her brief stay at the plantation, she'd loathed him at times, wanting to punch him for refusing to give in to her demands when she'd wanted to help catch A. D. Romero. But as much as he'd angered her with his obstinate determination, he also excited her in a way no other man had.

She had tried to overcome her lack of desire for men, which, rationally, she knew was due to the abuse A.D. and Wayne Romero had inflicted on her as a teen. But all of those attempts had failed. She'd come to realize that she simply had a fear of trusting men, and more than that, a fear of love. She'd loved her parents…and they'd died. She'd loved Lillian…and she'd been murdered. There was nothing that could be done to remedy that fear. Everyone she'd ever truly loved had been taken from her; she wouldn't let that happen again.

But there was no reason for her not to experience what other women enjoyed with men, true sexual pleasure. She just hadn't felt a desire for sex, until her time with Tristan at the plantation. Since then, she'd longed for it, burned for it, wanted to know everything that she'd missed…and she wanted to learn about it all with him. If any man could take her beyond her fear, it was Tristan.

Her teeth grazed her lower lip again.

"Chantelle, is something wrong?"

"I need your help…" She paused, glancing around them to ensure that no one was close enough to hear.

He moved nearer. How could she have such a fear of men in general, yet want this man more than her next breath? She swallowed, examining emerald-green eyes, the full mouth, the sexy dark waves teasing his temple. And wearing that tuxedo…Tristan looked good in his fireman's clothes, but in the tuxedo, he was downright transfixing. Her heart thundered against her ribs. If she had any doubts before, she had none now. She wanted him, in every sense of the word. And she didn't want to wait any longer.

"Chantelle, what do you need? Just tell me, and I'll do my best to help."

"You haven't heard what I need yet," she reminded him, and forced a quivering smile.

"Doesn't matter. If I can help you, I will. What do you want me to do?"

She swallowed, then stepped even closer, so close that she could feel raw male heat radiating from him. Then she whispered, "I want you…to sleep with me."

1

Five months later

CHANTELLE SAT IN HER CAR and fiddled with her keys while staring at the door to her apartment. She'd loved the place when she first saw it, and the location was perfect, on Magazine Street in New Orleans. She'd liked her previous house, a rental in a nice Metairie subdivision, but after A. D. Romero had attacked Kayla in that house, Chantelle simply couldn't go back. Besides, the Magazine Street apartment was perfect. While she was the only tenant under fifty in the complex, she didn't mind. Though her neighbors would be deemed nosy by most, Chantelle welcomed their inquisitiveness. It allowed her to never feel totally alone.

Chantelle hated to be alone.

The quaint complex was near the Garden District, where old New Orleans was new again, and also near the homeless shelter where Jenee Vicknair volunteered. Chantelle helped out at the shelter every now and then; it was a way to not only honor her sister, who had died beside it, but also to visit with Jenee and keep up with the Vicknair family—and Tristan.

He'd been on her mind lately. Or rather, he'd pretty

much dominated her thoughts for the past five months, ever since Dax's wedding, when she propositioned him to sleep with her, and he'd given her a night that she simply couldn't forget.

Tristan had held nothing back in their lovemaking. Unfortunately she hadn't been able to do the same. He'd touched her not only physically, but also emotionally, bringing her to tears—and scaring her enough that she'd left the next morning without so much as a proper goodbye.

That night he'd nearly conquered her fear of men. Nearly. She'd felt her body getting oh-so-close to letting go, but even with Tristan Vicknair, the only man she'd ever truly wanted, the memories of her past had invaded her attempt at finding pleasure with a man. So she'd pretended, put on an act, because it was easier to act as if she was normal, as if she hadn't been damaged in the past, than to admit the truth....

After that night, she feared that she may never be rid of the ghosts from her past.

And now, she was also unable to rid herself of the real honest-to-goodness ghost haunting her present.

As if on cue, the car grew colder. New Orleans was never what one would call cold, especially not at the end of May, but it was chilly tonight. Or was that simply her fear getting the best of her? Was *he* in her apartment again? And what would she do if he was?

She shivered as her blood passed through her veins. She'd thought about relocating again, somewhere far away from New Orleans and the pain of her past. But Ms. Rosa, the woman who'd cared for her during her teen years at the orphanage, had worked hard to find this place for her, and at a rental rate far below market value, because Chantelle had needed a little help getting on her feet after Lillian's death. She'd wanted to start over and pursue her dream of writing, and getting such a great deal on this place had given her that opportunity. And Chantelle was definitely back on her feet now; her first advance check for her novel had been a pleasant surprise, and the book's success even more shocking. She'd submitted it to a small press in New Orleans, and they'd wasted no time putting *Stuck in the Middle Realm* on local shelves. It wasn't on the *New York Times* list or anything like that, but New Orleans tourists—and locals—had really connected with the story based on Lillian's death, and Chantelle couldn't have been more pleased.

She'd simply followed Lillian's final piece of sisterly advice: pursue her dream of writing and live life to its fullest. Chantelle had written about what was close to her heart at the time, communicating with Lillian while she was in the middle realm. During her stay at the Vicknair plantation, she had learned plenty about the other side, and she'd taken that knowledge and turned it into a fictional account of a ghost who was trapped between the land of the living and the land of the dead. The book's unique premise had propelled it into a quick release, a nice print run and, basically, its becoming a local bestseller.

In her book, a beautiful ghost, Lorelei, can't cross over until she learns to trust someone enough to let them help her find the light. That someone—a medium named Evan—provided a romantic element to the plot that Chantelle truly hadn't anticipated when she began writing the book. But she knew Lorelei's inability to trust Evan reflected her own inability to trust men—to trust Tristan.

Unfortunately, though, based on her conversations with Jenee and Kayla, the Vicknair family was less than pleased that Chantelle had written something that so closely resembled the truth—their truth. And revealed their secrets. Jenee said that while she understood that Chantelle needed to write about something close to her heart and realized that no one would peg Evan as a fictitious member of the Vicknair family, the remainder of the family—particularly Nanette—didn't see it that way. They were simply waiting for the other shoe to drop, such as the media showing up outside their house one day and proclaiming it a freak house.

Kayla had been more positive in her assessment, saying the family simply needed time to realize that no one would have any reason to suspect their part in the story. Chantelle put more stock in Jenee's interpretation. However, ever since Chantelle had confided in her about her attempt to make love with Tristan, Kayla wasn't about to say anything that would upset her friend. But Chantelle sure hadn't intended to bring any trouble to Tristan or his family, and she honestly didn't think she had.

Jenee was right; she had simply written about something near and dear to her heart, and the next time she saw them—if she ever saw all of them again—she'd tell them that. She'd planned to tell Tristan personally when he'd left her a message to call him earlier this year. She'd called him back…but then she'd lost her nerve and hung up without even leaving a message. What would she say, anyway, to the guy she'd literally left after a one-night stand? Even worse, a one-night stand *she'd* initiated? She had next-to-no experience with decent men, and she certainly didn't have experience with how to treat one after sneaking out on him the morning after.

Chantelle recalled a comment from her editor when the woman had told Chantelle that the first few chapters for her second book appeared even more promising than the first book and that she could foresee Chantelle's "being a continual bestseller and never having another problem in the world."

But Chantelle did have problems, significant problems, including the one currently haunting her apartment—and her life. It was one thing to realize that ghosts had the ability to stay on this side until they were ready to cross, but it was something else entirely to have one personally haunting you, scaring you, making you afraid for your *own* life. Now she was truly second-guessing her decision to write about spirits; obviously this one had taken serious offense to her book. But what about Evan and Lorelei's story could have ticked off a ghost this much?

The knob on the radio in her car turned on its own, regardless of the fact that she held the keys in her hand, and the thing started playing "Unchained Melody." Then the locks on the doors all clicked into place—and a frisson of pure terror shot down her spine.

He hadn't bothered her outside of her apartment before, and she now realized that she'd erroneously assumed that meant she was safe outside of those walls. But she wasn't. He was here, and she was trapped—*trapped*—in her car.

"No!" She slammed her palms against her window.

It didn't matter. The street was empty, and even if anyone was nearby, she suspected they wouldn't come rushing to the aid of a woman who appeared to have locked herself in her vehicle and then started screaming about it.

She tried to get out, but the door wouldn't budge. Even so, she grabbed the icy handle and shook it hard enough to make the metal inside rattle eerily. Her breath coming out in harsh puffs of fog, she pried her fingers beneath the lock and attempted to force its release, only to find it was cemented in its current position.

As her panic increased, the music grew louder and louder, and she closed her eyes to try to combat the deafening sound. This ghost used the same tune for her torture every time. When he'd haunted her apartment, "Unchained Melody" had blasted from her radio until she'd finally smashed the radio this morning in an attempt to control the madness.

Had *that* ticked him off enough to make him come out here and confine her to the car?

Like every other time, Chantelle saw the vision that always emerged with this song—Patrick Swayze and Demi Moore, their hands entwined as they sat behind a pottery wheel with soft, wet clay oozing between their fingers as the two of them began to make love.

What was this ghost trying to tell her? Had he been taken from his lover? Was he trying to get her back? And why had he picked Chantelle to torment? Because of her fictional lovers? Chantelle had ended the book with an epilogue that catapulted to the future, when Evan died of old age—and found out that Lorelei had been waiting faithfully for him on the other side throughout his lifetime. Why would *that* upset this ghost? Was he tired of waiting for his lover to cross?

She listened to the music, blasting even louder. Patrick Swayze's character was murdered. Had this ghost been murdered? And what did he expect her to do about it?

"Let me out," Chantelle whispered. "Please."

The music continued to increase in volume, until the windows of the car vibrated with it, and Chantelle couldn't hold her tears back anymore. She'd worked so hard to finally have some semblance of control in her life, and this ghost was effectively taking that away, terrorizing her on a daily basis. She sobbed loudly, painfully, the despair of her situation gripping her as completely as fear gripped her soul. When she exhaled, her warm breath was cloudlike within the icy car.

She had no doubt now that the frigid temperature only existed around her; New Orleans wasn't this cold—ever—but this ghost certainly was, and he wanted to chill her, to freeze her to the bone.

He was succeeding.

She *hated* fear. She'd hated it since she was a teenager and had been forced to live with the emotion every day, fearing the dark, fearing those men, fearing that wretched knife against her throat, fearing…life itself.

Did the ghost know about that? Was her past a part of this? Or was this torment because of her book?

More important, how could she stop it?

Chantelle didn't know, but she had to find out. She simply couldn't live this way any longer. Slowly but surely, this ghost was driving her mad.

"Let me out," she pleaded again. "I'll do something.

I'll try to find whatever you need, try to help you and fix what's wrong. But you have to let me out!"

The music immediately ceased. Then the locks clicked loudly as they disengaged.

Chantelle opened the door, tumbled to the ground and was met with the blissful warmth of New Orleans. She stared at her car; the windows had fogged over with the contrasting temperature. A wave of exhaustion washed over her, and she knew that he'd left—for now. It had only been three days since she'd first sensed him, and that time had been merely a tingle at the back of her neck, an odd feeling like she was being watched. But with each visit, she felt more. Either she was becoming more perceptive or he was growing stronger.

No, regardless of whether she was becoming more perceptive or not, he was definitely growing stronger. This time, he'd shown up outside the apartment and had even managed to lock her in her car. In spite of the thick New Orleans heat, she shivered, wondering what else he could do.

Chantelle didn't attempt to get up; she still felt way too disoriented to even try. A *ghost* had the ability to trap her. Another man—a *dead* man—had found a way to abuse her. Not in the way she'd been abused as a teenager, but still…he'd made her stay in that car until *he* decided to let her go. Made her do something she didn't want to do. She'd vowed that would never happen again, yet it was happening nonetheless.

That infuriated her.

She didn't know for sure that her specter was a male, but she sensed a masculine presence every time the ghost was near and would wager that her personal haunter was most certainly male.

"Where are you now?" she whispered. "And what do you want?"

A door snapped closed, and she turned her head to see one of her elderly neighbors, Sundra Williams, exiting her apartment with her dog leading the way. The woman gasped, then rushed toward Chantelle. Her dog, a silver toy poodle named Beignet, got to Chantelle first and started licking her cheek.

Chantelle turned her head away from the busy little tongue, while the woman shooed Beignet away.

"No, no, Beignet. Oh, dear, oh, my, did you fall?" The woman's knees cracked loudly as she bent over Chantelle and gingerly tried to ease her to a sitting position. She pushed Chantelle's long, blond curls behind her shoulders, gently tucking a wayward strand behind her right ear. "Poor dear."

"I'm okay, Mrs. Williams."

The woman placed the back of her hand against Chantelle's forehead, and her eyes grew wide behind her round, silver-framed glasses. "No, you're not okay. You're burning up, child. Let's get you inside, and I'll find something to help with that fever."

Burning up? Chantelle was freezing. "Fever?"

"Yes, dear. Now, come on, let's get you inside." In spite of her tiny frame, she took Chantelle's hands and actually pulled her to her feet, while Beignet nipped at the hem of Chantelle's jeans.

"I'll be okay, Mrs. Williams." But she allowed the woman to guide her to her apartment, then fished her key from her jeans and focused on sliding it into the lock. She had no idea whether her personal haunter was on the other side of the door, and she didn't want to scare Mrs. Williams if he was. "You can go on home. I'll be okay."

"Nonsense," the woman said, ushering Chantelle inside and steering her to the couch. "Now you wait right here, and I'll go get some aspirin from my place."

Chantelle surveyed her surroundings and prayed that her ghost wasn't here. "I've got some in the kitchen cabinet," she said. "To the left of the sink."

Her neighbor nodded primly. In a matter of seconds, she and Beignet returned from Chantelle's kitchen with a cup of water and two pills. "Take these, dear."

Chantelle did as Mrs. Williams instructed and found it oddly comforting to be cared for by the older woman. True, there was nothing physically wrong with her; she'd simply been spooked by a persistent ghost. But she hadn't had anyone take care of her since she left Ms. Rosa and the orphanage, and this was very…nice.

"Thank you."

"Well, I'm not sure what's going on, my dear, but you need a little old-fashioned TLC. Too bad you don't have a nice young man in your life to give you that." She slowly added, "My grandson is coming into town for a visit next month. Maybe the two of you can—"

"No," Chantelle said quickly, then improvised, "I'm really too busy for dating right now." It was a lie, sort of, unless you counted the fact that her personal ghost was keeping her busy by scaring her to death. She really wasn't ready to try the dating thing. She'd given up after her night with Tristan. If any guy could have done it for her, it'd have to have been that beautiful tribute to

Acadian ancestry. But there were way too many ghosts in her life now, both from the past and the present, to fit a living man into the picture.

"Well, we'll see when it's closer to the time of Tim's visit. In any case, Beignet and I are perfectly willing to stay here and take care of you…but if you'd rather we leave, that's fine."

"I'm sure I'll be okay on my own, but thank you for offering to stay." Chantelle felt better merely talking to her neighbor, even if there was a good chance her ghostly visitor would eventually return.

"Young women your age don't typically fall out of their cars, and you certainly shouldn't be lying in a parking lot with a raging fever. I do wish you had someone to take care of you, dear. Someone besides an old lady and her dog." She tilted her head, then asked, "How old are you?"

"How old am I?"

"Yes, dear," Mrs. Williams said in an almost reprimanding tone. "How old are you?"

"Twenty-three."

"I suspected you were in your early twenties. So tell me, what *is* a successful, pretty girl like you doing living here all alone, staying by yourself all of the time and not socializing any that I've seen? It's Friday night, and yet here you are, all by your lonesome." She tsked. "Doesn't make sense to me. You need someone in your life, dear. You know, I've got a doctor friend. You wouldn't even have to wait until Tim comes to visit to meet somebody nice. I'll call him—I think you two might just hit it off, and he could come over right now and check on that fever too."

"No," Chantelle said again with a bit more assertiveness than before. She did not want to be fixed up with anyone, particularly a "doctor friend."

"Why not?"

Why not? Well, that was a good question. What was the answer? That she didn't want to get anything started with anyone, since she was currently dealing with an irritated specter and didn't want to confuse the issue with a relationship? Or should she tell the woman that she didn't want to start anything with anyone, because she'd already had—and left—the only one she'd ever wanted?

And why *had* she left Tristan without looking back? He obviously wasn't the one with the problem. Maybe if they tried again, things would be different. And maybe he hadn't even realized that she was dealing with her hang-ups during their night together. He hadn't said anything.

"If you aren't going to let me introduce you to Dr. Marvy and let him help you to get better—and I mean get better in several aspects of the word—then I want you to promise me that you'll ask someone else for help. Help toward getting you better physically, and help toward fixing whatever keeps you living in a place with a bunch of old fogies when you should be enjoying the prime of your life. Promise me, dear, that you'll call someone."

Chantelle could only think of one person to call.

"Will you?" her neighbor asked, relentless in her goal to elicit the answer she wanted.

The truth was, Chantelle did need help. She couldn't deal with this spirit on her own, and she needed to talk to someone who had expertise in dealing with ghosts. But while Tristan was the person who came to mind, she wasn't ready to see him again. What did you say to a guy you'd propositioned and then left while he was still sleeping? How would she explain? And would he forgive her if she did?

"Will you?" Mrs. Williams repeated. "Because I could still call Dr. Marvy."

No, she couldn't call Tristan. She just couldn't. But he wasn't the only person she knew who dealt with spirits on a regular basis. There were several Vicknairs in the bunch, and any of them would know more about this than she did. Besides, it was probably high time she explained to all of them that she hadn't meant to cause any harm with her book.

"I will."

2

"MON DIEU, she must be really something," Liana Chenevert said, her chocolate-colored eyes peering at Tristan over the top of her margarita.

"Who?"

"The woman who's been on your mind all night, and hell, all year. I may have had you in my bed a time or two since that Mardi Gras party, and while your body was into it, the mind was anywhere but." She licked salt from the rim of her glass before taking a sip, moved her shoulders in a way that pushed her boobs up front and center in her skimpy green dress, then smiled. "Gotta tell you that even when your mind's not in it, you're better than most, but I'm not sure that I want to sleep with you again if there's going to be a ghost in the bed."

Tristan downed the rest of his beer. A ghost in the bed. Funny way of putting it, since he dealt with ghosts regularly—them he could handle—but Chantelle Bedeau was anything but a ghost. She was alive and well, and definitely nowhere near Tristan's bed. She'd only been there once, nearly six months ago, a fact that tormented him daily. And he could point out to Liana that he hadn't *asked* her to sleep with him tonight, or any other night since they'd first hooked up at Ryan and

Monique's Mardi Gras party. Sure, he'd tried to get Chantelle off his mind with an excess of women in his bed, Liana included, for a while—but he'd finally realized that no other woman was going to fill the void Chantelle had left when she'd asked him to "help her," then left him cold.

More than that, he suspected he'd left her unfulfilled throughout their entire heated encounter. The failure still ate at him.

"Remy, give me another," Tristan called to the bartender, while Liana shimmied closer.

"So, you wanna come to my place, or do you want me to come to yours?" She leaned toward his ear. "Doesn't really matter—either way, we both come." Then she giggled, while Tristan accepted his next beer and frowned.

"Sorry, Liana. Not tonight."

Her over-glossed lips puckered in a frown that he was certain she'd practiced in front of a mirror, it was such a perfect example of what his Creole ancestors had termed a *bahbin*. And he'd bet it worked nearly as well as his cousin Monique's pout, getting her practically everything she wanted in life. Too bad for Liana Tristan was immune to the effect.

"Oh, come on, Tristan. I don't care if your mind's somewhere else." She ran her hand up his thigh on a direct path to his crotch, and Tristan promptly slid off the bar stool before she started working her magic on his cock.

"Not tonight, Liana," he repeated, then nodded his goodbye and headed to the back of the bar, where several of his firefighting buddies were spending their night off shooting pool.

"No way," Gerry Breaux said, racking up for a game of 8-ball. "You turned Liana down again? Hell, that's one hot woman, Chief. I can guar-an-tee I wouldn't turn that black-haired Cajun down. No way, no how."

"We haven't found one yet that you'd turn down, Breaux," Marc Farrell retorted, then shifted his gaze to Tristan. "But I've gotta tell you, Vicknair, the women *are* talking. My sister even asked me about you."

Tristan's ears perked up at that. Marc's sister, Alyssa, was one of the first women he slept with after Chantelle's disappearing act. She and Tristan had been friends for years, but had only slept together that once, when his heart was bruised and his cock was aching. They'd decided that it was a mistake—he'd admitted his mind was on someone else, and so had she—and then they'd agreed to keep things at the friendship level.

So what was she saying to her brother, to one of *his* firefighters, no less?

"Alyssa said that she thought you were hooked on someone, but then she said you never showed up with the same woman twice, and then you just stopped showing up with women, period. Hell, you know I feel funny asking, but since we're in the same house and all," Marc Ferrell said, referring to the LaPlace fire station where they worked, "we're still playing for the same team, right?"

"Whoa now," Gerry interjected. "The chief? Vicknair? Are you serious? No way in hell."

"Got that right," Tristan drawled, holding his beer bottle up in mock salute.

"Then what gives?" Marc asked. "We haven't seen you with a skirt in—what's it been?—a couple of months? And every one of us just watched you turn down a woman who'd do you on this pool table if you'd let her."

"Ask Liana," Tristan said, deciding against pool for tonight. He didn't need to take this shit, and he sure didn't feel like making excuses for losing his head and his heart to a woman who didn't want him for more than a one-night stand. And the only woman he hadn't been able to bring to orgasm. Hell, he'd bet a month's salary that she'd faked it. Dammit. "Liana will tell you."

"What's she gonna tell us?" Gerry asked as Tristan headed for the door.

Tristan turned, set his empty beer bottle on the counter, then smirked. "That I've got a ghost in my bed."

He exited the bar, somewhat disappointed that he didn't even have a buzz from his efforts.

No buzz off the beer. No sex from Liana. No pool with the guys.

Another thrilling night in the neighborhood.

A year ago, he'd have downed more beer, won the majority of the games of pool and taken Liana home for a good ride—or four—in the sack. But then, he'd met Chantelle. And then, he'd slept with Chantelle.

And then…his life had gone to hell.

He wanted her, literally ached to have her again, and also wanted to prove to her that he could get her where she needed to go *if* she'd give him another shot. But hell, he wasn't into begging, either. He'd called her once— once—after her disappearing act. She hadn't returned the call, and he'd sworn he wouldn't make the same mistake again. He wasn't exactly hurting for opportunity. But he was hurting for her, which really pissed him off. He wanted her, but he also despised her for leaving him wanting more.

He could still see her blond hair, falling as he removed the tiny pins holding it in place, the way it had cascaded past her shoulders and tumbled past her full breasts. He could still remember the way her nipples budded into firm hard peaks before he'd even touched them. And the way her entire body had trembled, on the verge of letting go.

On the verge. She'd been there, so close, and she'd cried out as though losing control. But even though he'd wanted to believe she'd let go for him that night, the more he thought about the way she'd acted before, during and after, the more Tristan knew he'd been played.

She hadn't come. Not three times, as she'd pretended, or even once. And unfortunately, no matter how often he remembered that night, the primary memory that overshadowed everything else was the next morning, when he awoke with a contented smile on his face and found her gone.

He inhaled the warm night air and smelled a hint of smoke. Scanning the area around him, he knew there wasn't a fire nearby, and he also knew that the scent wasn't his clothing. He kept his work clothes at the firehouse and his off-duty clothing at home. No, this scent was the result of something else entirely.

A ghost was on the way.

The Vicknair mediums all had calling cards for when they were going to receive a spirit. Since the majority of Tristan's specters lost their lives in fires, he either heard the crackling of a burning fire or smelled smoke, like now.

He took another deep breath, but the familiar scent was gone. That sometimes happened, a sign that the spirit was on the way, but it might take a while. Good. Tristan was tired and frustrated, and could use a night of sleep before he had to help another ghost find the light.

He crossed the wooden bridge that led to his apartment. The water in the canal below took on a different appearance on nights like this, losing its traditional murkiness and actually sparkling beneath the moonlight. The last time he'd seen a moon this bright had been the night of Dax's wedding—the night he'd made love to Chantelle. He recalled walking Chantelle across this very bridge with the water sparkling like this, leaning her against the railing and tasting her lips for the very first time.

"Damn." He'd been a fool. Throughout his adulthood, he'd always made sure the women he dated knew the way things stood. He enjoyed them, thoroughly, but he wasn't about to lead any of them on. He didn't want to get tied down; he wanted to have fun. But that wasn't the entire reason he didn't settle down; the truth was, he had the Vicknair legacy to deal with, and like it or not, any woman who ended up with a Vicknair would also get the family's uncanny ability to communicate with ghosts. Not exactly something he could proudly make known during the dating process.

With Chantelle, he didn't have to tell her about their family secrets; she already knew. And maybe because of that, he'd let his guard down and lost himself in her sky-blue eyes, her heart-shaped mouth, her heated touch. He'd been completely into her that night, and she'd been…unfulfilled.

Was it because of her past? Because of the abuse? That was what he suspected, but why didn't she let him know? Why hadn't she given him the chance to help her move past those barriers, instead of leaving him wondering what he did wrong?

Truthfully, he'd been mesmerized by her ever since they'd tangled at the plantation, fighting and fussing about practically everything from the moment she arrived, two headstrong individuals who didn't like to back down. He wasn't used to anyone but Nan giving him that kind of resistance. The guys at the station joked around with him, but no one questioned his authority or truly stood toe-to-toe with him, ever. Chantelle, however, did. That had only caused him to be even more infatuated with her.

Hell, who was he kidding? He'd been infatuated with everything about her, and he'd given her everything he had to offer…and she had walked away.

Lesson learned. Don't put your heart out there and it won't get trampled by an intriguing blue-eyed blonde.

He entered his apartment and immediately smelled more smoke. A surge of adrenaline flooded through him, the way it always did when he approached a fire, but a brief scan of the place told him that, once again, this wasn't ordinary smoke. His grandmother was letting him know that his ghost would be here sooner than he thought. The scent was stronger than before and accompanied by the faintest sound of wood crackling and splintering from extreme heat.

Tristan could almost feel that heat, could almost sense the power of it claiming the ghost's soul. There'd been a fire in Gramercy last night, and a thirty-five-year-old man, Jake Laberdie, had been critically injured. Tristan had been there and had seen firsthand the extent of Laberdie's injuries. The last time Tristan had checked, the man had been hanging on in the critical-care unit at Ochsner Hospital, where Tristan's cousin Gage worked. Maybe he should call Gage and check on Jake Laberdie's condition, not that it would change anything. If it was time for the man to go to the other side, he would. And if Tristan was chosen as the medium to help him cross, assuming Jake needed help, then he would do his job.

But the smoke, once again, began to dissipate. Perhaps Jake Laberdie, or whoever the spirit was, was hovering between life and death. Occasionally, Tristan would sense a spirit teetering between the two sides, and then either he'd receive one of his grandmother's letters in the sitting room of the Vicknair plantation house, or the smoke would go away completely, signaling the spirit had returned completely to the land of the living.

Tristan took a quick shower, then fell into bed, determined to force his mind to relax and gain some much needed sleep.

His mind, however, had other plans. His night was filled with heated, passionate dreams of Chantelle Bedeau, her blue eyes glazed over, her mouth opened in orgasmic bliss, her body alive and on fire and letting go—really letting go—at his command.

It was a dream that he'd give anything to make a reality.

3

CHANTELLE MANEUVERED her car along the winding curves that bordered the mighty Mississippi, the levee on her left and a conglomeration of housing extremes on her right. A mobile home nudged up against a plantation house, which overshadowed a modern colonial, which banked against a shack. Oddly enough, the bizarre assortment only added to the appeal of River Road.

She'd decided against calling Nanette Vicknair last night, because there was no way she could have avoided sounding panicked, phoning late on a Friday evening to say that her apartment was haunted and that the ghost had also made an appearance in her car. She knew Nan would believe her; she was a Vicknair, after all, and ghosts were nothing out of the ordinary for any member of that family. But she didn't want to appear out of control.

Chances were, Chantelle's ghost was simply stuck in the middle, knew that she had some experience with spirits due to her book and wanted her to help him find his way to the light. He needed a medium, and while Chantelle knew about mediums, she wasn't one, and she sure didn't know what to tell this spirit to do in order to cross. So she was driving to the Vicknair plantation to ask Nanette, the oldest medium of the lot, to help get this ghost headed in the right direction—and away from Chantelle's apartment, car and life.

Granted, a phone call could have taken care of the conversation with Nan, but Chantelle still wasn't all that certain exactly how upset Nan was with her for writing her book and wanted to explain in person that she'd never betray their family secret. Plus, she missed the Vicknairs. She hadn't visited them much at all since Dax's wedding and that awkward night with Tristan, and spending some time with them at the plantation would make for a nice Saturday—if they were no longer upset over the book.

She wondered what Tristan thought of it. Jenee had never said, and Chantelle would've felt strange asking her about her brother's opinion. And Kayla had said she'd never heard him comment one way or another.

Tristan didn't live at the family home; he had an apartment in LaPlace, near the fire station. Chances were she wouldn't even see him today.

She neared the driveway leading to the Vicknair plantation house and chewed her lower lip. Who was she kidding? She knew that all the Vicknairs came to the family home every Saturday for their traditional workday. They'd been doing that ever since Katrina had battered the plantation, along with the rest of Louisiana. The parish president, Charles Roussel, was head of the committee that determined which homes were an environmental hazard after the hurricane, and for some reason he had been trying to move the Vicknair plantation house to the top of the list for demolition ever since the storm. For the past two years the family had continually jumped through

Roussel's hoops to save their home. Chantelle knew it was a long-term project and one that would last presumably until the end of this year. Therefore, she knew that they'd be here today, all of them, including the tall, muscled fireman whose tempting waves of dark hair teased her fingers, whose vivid green eyes made her insides quiver and whose kiss left her weak-kneed.

She rolled her window down to inhale the magnolias, blooming boldly on the towering trees, miraculously spared in the storm, which bordered the driveway. Then she eased the car toward the house, where sedans and Jeeps and trucks were parked sporadically on the driveway that circled a huge oak. Too many cars for just the Vicknair family.

Her heartbeat stepped up a notch. She wanted to talk to the Vicknairs, particularly Nanette, about her ghostly problem, but she didn't want to divulge it to the masses. Who all was here, anyway? Chantelle spotted men, lots of men, all wearing navy T-shirts and jeans, carrying tools and climbing ladders on the right side of the vast columned home. She didn't spot a Vicknair in the group, but then again, it'd be hard to pick one out in the crowd of men. There had to be at least twenty, maybe even thirty, busily clambering around the house and apparently removing a large portion of the siding. Wood was flung through the air and landed in a growing pile.

She slowed her car to a crawl as she circled the oak, trying to find a place to park—and the air around her grew cold.

It didn't matter that her window was down and the usual Louisiana heat had been stifling mere moments ago. Right now, everything was icy, and she knew why. He was here.

"No."

As soon as she spoke, the presence applied pressure to her leg. Her right knee was pushed downward, making her foot press the gas pedal and her car accelerate out of control.

"No!" Chantelle barely registered the men yelling when her tires kicked up gravel and sent a cloud of dust behind her as she surged forward. She saw the red fire-department car in time to twist the steering wheel and miss it, but the pedal remained pressed to the floor, the speed increasing as she rounded the side of the house and shot toward the cane field. She gripped the wheel more tightly and fought to pull her foot away, but the pressure on her leg intensified, sending a rush of sheer pain up her thigh. She screamed, then the wheel turned sharply, and the large shed at the rear of the Vicknair property grew closer, and closer, until the car violently slammed through the side, and everything went black.

TRISTAN PEELED AWAY another piece of rotted siding and tossed it toward the steadily growing pile that would have to be hauled away later. Every fireman who wasn't on duty had shown up this morning; their generosity never failed to amaze him. The group volunteered their time each Saturday to help restore homes that had been damaged by Katrina, and one Saturday of every month found them all here at the Vicknair place, helping his family. Proof that firemen truly were as close as brothers, there for each other in times of happiness and times of trouble. Sure, there'd been quite a bit of colorful language throughout the morning, when they encountered a stubborn obstacle in their path to repairing the structural damage on the right side of the house, where hurricane Katrina had basically pushed the frame inward and nearly toppled the beloved home. But they never wavered in their efforts, giving all they had on a day when they'd probably rather be chilling at home or fishing on the bayou.

The gravel crunching on the driveway was his first clue that one of the guys was making a late arrival, a very late arrival, given they'd started working at six that morning and it was well after noon now. He squinted toward the silver Volkswagen Beetle as it neared. He didn't recognize it and didn't think it belonged to any of his men. After it cleared the shade of the magnolias and started circling the big oak, the sun finally shone through the windshield to illuminate the driver, with her long, blond curls tumbling past her shoulders.

It was no fireman, and it wasn't any of their wives, either. Tristan knew the woman behind the wheel. He had no idea what she was doing here, but his speeding pulse said that the reason didn't matter. Chantelle Bedeau *was* here, and he was going to talk to her, to settle this thing once and for all.

Maybe then he wouldn't dream about her every night.

Maybe then he'd have her beside him every night.

Or maybe he'd throttle her for leaving him that particular night and not even bothering to return his call.

He'd only made it halfway down the ladder when he heard tires spinning against the gravel and then her ear-piercing scream.

"Hell, what's happening?" Gerry Breaux yelled from the front porch.

"She's going to crash!" someone shouted.

Tristan jumped the rest of the way to the ground, then ran around the side of the house in time to see Chantelle's Beetle swerve wildly, tires spinning, dust flying, as it picked up speed, then rammed into the shed.

Nanette and Jenee bolted out the back door of the house in front of Tristan, but he sprinted past them and got to the car first.

"Oh, no!" Jenee gasped.

"Who is it?" Nan asked, nearing Tristan, Gerry and Marc, the first three guys to reach the car.

"Chantelle, are you okay?" Tristan yelled, climbing over the splintered debris from the shed doors and making his way to the driver's side, which, thank goodness, appeared intact.

"It's Chantelle," Jenee said, standing behind the car while more firemen moved in to help. "Is she okay?"

"Chantelle!" Tristan repeated, opening her door.

She moaned, but her eyes remained closed and she didn't make any effort to move. The deployed airbag covered the top half of her body. He lifted the bag and hurriedly scanned the steering wheel to see if it was bent. If it was, she most certainly would have internal injuries.

The wheel was intact. Thank God.

White talcum powder, released when the airbag deployed, covered the front seat and Chantelle. Apparently having inhaled some, she coughed softly, then frowned, her eyes still closed.

"Chantelle, can you hear me? It's Tristan. I'm going to help you." He fought for the required composure that he used when tending to any accident victim, even if this particular victim was anything but the norm.

What was she doing here? And why in the hell had she steered her car into the shed?

Gerry pulled the passenger door open and crawled in, then immediately started moving the airbag out of the way so he and Tristan could properly assess her injuries. "What you got?" he asked Tristan.

Chantelle's eyes fluttered, and she squinted at Gerry. "He's here?" she asked.

"Who?" Gerry responded while Tristan leaned closer to her.

"Chantelle, does anything hurt?" Tristan breathed a sigh of relief when she slowly shook her head, then turned those sky-blue eyes on him. He tried to concentrate on his training; in this case, first-responder training, specifically crash extrication. However, all the training in the world never prepared you for the injured person being someone you knew, someone you cared about. He *needed* to verify that she was okay, but he *wanted* to hold her, comfort her, kiss her.

"Tristan?"

Thank God, his training kicked back in. *The injured person is conscious. Explain to her what happened and what you are going to do.* "Yes. You had an accident. We need to get you out of here and check for injuries." He looked at Gerry. "Go bring the station car over. We'll take her to Ochsner."

She coughed again. "No. I don't need to be checked out. I'm not going to the hospital. What if he went there, too? And I'm not hurt. I just need you to get rid of him." She gave another cough.

"Who?" Tristan asked.

She shook her head, then tried to sit forward, but her seat belt wouldn't budge. "It's stuck."

That was the Chantelle he knew, refusing to listen to his request because it wasn't what she wanted to hear, and bossing him around.

"I got it," Gerry said, pulling out a knife. Effortlessly, he sliced through the nylon strap and freed her, but Chantelle no longer cared. She trembled all over, sucked in an audible breath, then started coughing again. "Put it away," she said hoarsely, staring at the knife. Then she added, "Please. Please put it away."

Gerry apologized, shrugged confusedly, then tucked the knife back in his pocket before leaving the car.

"I'm not going to the hospital," she repeated, then squirmed around to move her legs out of the vehicle. "You can't take me if I say no, and I say no. I can't go there now. I need to talk to Nanette, or, I guess, all of you."

"Let me through, please." Gage's voice got Tristan's attention, and he turned to see his cousin pushing past Jenee and Nanette with Kayla, his wife, following in his wake. Gage had worked all night in the ER and had planned to arrive late to help with the plantation-house repairs. Tristan was glad he'd arrived earlier than anticipated. Maybe Chantelle would listen to a doctor.

"When did you get here?" Tristan asked.

"Just now," Gage said, easing past Tristan and squatting in front of Chantelle. He put his hand on her chin and examined her pupils. "Chantelle, what happened?"

She moved her head away from his hand. "I couldn't

control him. I *can't* control him. And I need you—or some of the other Vicknairs—to get rid of him."

"Who?" Gage asked.

"My ghost."

4

CHANTELLE SAT at the long mahogany table in the Vicknairs' kitchen and sipped the strong Community coffee, while Nanette, Jenee, Dax, Celeste, Gage, Kayla *and* Tristan waited for her to speak. After she'd climbed from the car and refused to be treated for possible injuries—she was merely shaken, not hurt—they'd ushered her inside and insisted she sit down and try to gain her bearings.

Easier said than done.

Kayla sat beside Chantelle with her arm draped around her back. Chantelle swallowed the last of her coffee, then placed the empty cup on the table.

"Do you want another cup?" Kayla asked, her dark eyes etched with concern.

"No, but thanks." Chantelle stared at the cup rather than at everyone watching her so intently, particularly the man sitting across from her. Tristan's presence made her almost as uncomfortable as the ghost who'd tried to kill her, or at least harm her, a few minutes ago. "I'm sorry about your shed," she finally said to no one in particular. Then she decided, as long as she was apologizing… "And I'm sorry I upset you with my book."

Gage shrugged. "Hell, the shed needed an upgrade,

anyway. We'll just add that to the list of things to do. And I figure if your book was going to stir up trouble for us, it would've happened by now. No camera crew has shown up yet, so you're in the clear. Isn't that right, Nanette?"

Chantelle, and everyone else in the room, turned toward Nan, the oldest cousin and unofficial head of the family. Clothed in a black tank top and black work pants, she leaned forward in her seat next to Tristan, her mouth quirking to the side in a half frown as she waited a beat, then finally answered, "I admit I was upset when I first learned about the subject matter for the book, but I did read it, and you didn't say anything to betray our secret." She paused, then added, "Thank you for that."

"So I guess that's that," Dax said, chuckling, and Chantelle looked up, relieved to see all of them smiling. Well, all of them except Tristan, who was staring at her and making her feel even more ill at ease about her present situation.

A loud banging echoed through the house and reminded Chantelle of the firemen outside, working diligently on the home. In his usual take-charge manner, Tristan had told them that the family would help Chantelle. They'd simply nodded, accepting Tristan's undisputed authority, and returned to work. Now his intense green eyes were surveying her, and Chantelle remembered the way she'd felt that night when those gorgeous eyes were even more intense and filled with unbridled desire—for her.

Her skin tingled, as though she was unable to contain the magnitude of emotion, the burning hunger that instantly pulsed through her whenever he was near. To combat it, she turned her attention back to her near miss. How many of his firefighters had heard her ghost comment? And how many of them thought she was off her rocker? She *had* run her car into the shed and then asked them to get rid of her ghost. Not a lot of sanity displayed there.

"You said you need us to get rid of your ghost," Nanette prompted, apparently also deciding it was time to get down to the nitty-gritty. "Can we assume the car accident has something to do with that request?"

"Three days ago, a ghost showed up in my apartment," Chantelle said before she lost her nerve. She paused, expecting questions, but they merely waited to hear the rest. She inhaled, resolved that she had to tell them everything. "He didn't do anything big at first—turned on the television and caused the radio to play 'Unchained Melody,' even when it wasn't switched on. But I kept feeling like I was being watched, you know?"

Jenee nodded. "We know exactly. We sense that feeling almost all the—" She halted when an engine rumbled noisily from outside, and then a loud beeping signaled a truck was backing up.

"That'll be the tow truck," Dax noted, standing. "I'll go show them where your car is," he said to Chantelle.

"You think they won't figure out which one it is by the fact that it's halfway through the shed?" Gage asked, then grunted when Kayla elbowed him.

"Gage," she scolded, but her eyes said she wasn't mad, probably couldn't get mad, at her new husband.

"Sorry," he apologized, more to Chantelle than to his wife. "Bad joke."

"I'll go with Dax," Celeste said, and followed her

husband outside. "We'll make sure your car is taken care of."

Chantelle nodded. She was dismayed that she'd wrecked it, even if unintentionally. She loved the pretty silver Beetle, her one impulsive purchase when she'd gotten her advance check, and now the front end was crushed, having not only smashed into the shed, but also collided with the cane harvester just inside the metal doors.

"Tell us about the ghost." Tristan's words, more of a command than a request, caught her off-guard, but then again, that had been his way when she'd spent time with him here at the plantation last fall. However, when they'd slept together, he'd been the opposite—very receptive to her body's needs, to her natural response to his touch. He hadn't been demanding at all. No, he was almost…coaxing, gently taking her so very close to the edge. Yet she still hadn't been able to push herself over.

"You said you need us to get *him* to leave, so I'm assuming you're sure this isn't Lillian watching over you."

Chantelle inhaled, let the breath out slowly and decided against taking offense, for now. He was probably still ticked off by her departure the morning after they'd had sex, so she'd allow him one smart-ass remark, but if he did it again, she wasn't going to be nice. "It isn't Lillian. I do feel her watching over me every now and then, but this isn't like that. It's more, I don't know, dominating. Stronger. And determined."

"It could be a guy stuck in the middle the way Ryan was," Jenee said. "I wish he were here now, but Monique was having a time with her morning sickness, and they decided to stay home and take it easy until she's feeling better."

"Monique is pregnant?" Chantelle asked, just realizing that one of the Vicknairs wasn't present for the workday. Jenee was right; since Monique's husband, Ryan Chappelle, was a former spirit who had come back from the other side, he was the most likely to know something helpful about this male ghost who was apparently hovering in the middle and, for some reason, fixated on Chantelle. She'd make it a point to talk to him later, see if he could tell her anything about why this spirit might be tormenting her—and what she could do to make him leave.

"Three months along," Jenee said with a grin. "She's excited, even if she can't hold any food down until late afternoon."

"Who do you think it is?" Tristan asked, not swayed by the sidetrack in subject matter. "The ghost. Do you think it's someone you know?" He seemed determined to focus on the situation with her ghost, instead of on her. But she knew him well enough to see beneath the tough-guy exterior. He *was* focused on her, and right now he was feeling just as much tension as she did. They'd left things unfinished, but Tristan Vicknair wasn't the type of guy to let the uneasiness between them linger in the shadows. He'd bring it up front and center, haul it to the surface and force her to deal with what happened that night, and why she left the next morning. How long did she have before he did?

"Do you think it's someone you know?" he repeated.

Chantelle shook her head. "I don't think so. I believe he knows about my book, and because of it, he thinks

I can help him cross. That's why I wanted to talk to all of you. I think he needs a medium. I don't know how to send him here, but…"

"But?" Tristan's tone was once again clipped, his jaw firmly set and those green eyes slightly narrowed. Have mercy, he was still pissed off. Chantelle caught a glimpse of Kayla's mouth thinning; hopefully she was the only other person in the room aware of the mounting tension between them. Obviously Tristan wasn't used to women leaving him. Then again, what woman in her right mind would leave a guy who looked like that? And made love like that?

"Chantelle," he said, pulling her back to the here and now, and away from memories of him, naked and beautifully muscled, in bed. "But what?"

"But he came here with me today," she said, snapping back to reality. "So you'd think he would've picked up on the fact that ghosts come here. I mean, don't ghosts see each other? Don't they know where they all go to find a medium? That's the way it seemed to me when Ryan talked about it before, and that's the way I portrayed it in my book."

"Wait a minute," Nanette interrupted. "Your ghost came here today with you? Was he in the car with you when you crashed? Is that what happened? He showed up in the car and you sensed him and it spooked you?"

"No, it was more than that," Chantelle said as Dax and Celeste came through the back door.

"Paul Boudreaux said he'll phone when they assess the damage on the car," Dax told her.

"He didn't think it would take him all that long to

repair it," Celeste added. "He said just call him with your insurance information."

"Will you ask him just to repair it? I don't want it on my insurance." She'd had a perfect driving record until today and didn't want her rate to go up because a ghost had, essentially, wrecked her car. "I'll pay for it on my own."

"Okay, your call," Dax said, sitting at the table with Celeste. "What?" he asked, apparently picking up on the tension in the room, as everyone else remained silent, waiting for Chantelle to say more. "What's going on?"

"Chantelle's about to tell us what happened out there." Tristan's chair creaked as he scooted closer to the table and leaned toward Chantelle. "What do you mean, it was more than that? *Did* your ghost come with you? Did *he* spook you?"

"Yes, he did," she admitted. "He's been doing that, and I think I've been handling it pretty well. But today, when he showed up in my car, he wasn't just trying to spook me. I think—no, I'm sure—that he tried to hurt me."

"What?" they all said together, and Chantelle couldn't discern one voice from another.

Tristan's chair scraped against the tile floor as he straightened, his brows dipping sternly. "Tried to hurt you? Are you saying that a ghost drove your car into the shed?"

"No, I was definitely driving, but *something* pushed down my leg and made my foot press the accelerator. And when I tried to pull it off, the force got stronger, to the point of pain. I *couldn't* stop the car, and then he steered it straight into the shed." Chantelle was amazed at the relief she felt merely stating her problem out loud. There was definitely something to be said about passing on your burden, but from the look on Tristan's face, a look that said he wanted to hurt someone, she wasn't all that certain that passing her ghostly burden to this particular medium was such a good idea.

All of the Vicknairs started talking at once, each of them trying to recall whether they'd ever heard of a ghost trying to harm a person or even having the ability to force a person to do something they didn't want to do. Chantelle listened to their ponderings with interest, and then glanced at the only one who hadn't joined in.

Tristan was staring at her, his face unreadable.

"I'm fine now, though," she said, the words primarily for his benefit, though she stated them to the room. "And I just want to figure out how to get him to cross and to leave me alone."

"He hasn't been assigned to any of us," Nanette said. "The only one of us who has even had a spirit lately is Kayla, and her little girl crossed last night."

"Kayla?" Chantelle turned to her friend. "You helped a ghost cross?"

"After Gage and I married, I started getting spirits to help, too. I help little girls who've been abused."

Chantelle didn't need to ask why Kayla got those spirits; like her, she'd know plenty about being abused.

"Tristan, you said you have a ghost coming, though, didn't you?" Dax asked. "You've smelled smoke since last night, right?"

Tristan nodded. "I've got one coming, but I can't imagine why my ghost would want to harm Chantelle."

He paused a beat, then added, "But if you *have* got a ghost after you, we need to figure out why."

"That's why I came here."

"You said he showed up in your apartment three days ago?" Tristan asked. "Why didn't you call and let me know before now?"

She didn't miss the fact that he'd said "let *me* know" rather than "let *us* know."

"I honestly thought he'd go away, and I also thought he was confined to the apartment, until last night."

"What happened last night?" Jenee asked.

"He locked me in my car."

"He locked you in your car? Did he try to hurt you then, too?" Tristan's voice was deep, controlled—but barely. Chantelle got the distinct impression that if he could get his hands on her ghost right now, he'd kill him—again. "Did he try to hurt you?"

Chantelle felt more than a bit of irritation at how he made her feel as though she was being interrogated. She hadn't done anything wrong, after all. But since the rest of the family was also waiting for her response, she bit back the urge to snap at Tristan, and answered his question. "No, not really. The temperature dropped so low that the windows fogged, but that was it. After a while, he unlocked the doors and let me get out. It…shook me up a bit."

"I guess it did," Dax said. "And then what? He didn't show up again until today, when he caused you to crash the car?"

"Right. But that's what bothers me now. If he can make me do things like that, push my foot against the accelerator and force my hand to jerk the wheel, what else can he do? I mean, if he's intent on hurting me, what if he makes me…" She didn't want to finish the sentence, mainly because she didn't know how. What *could* he make her do? Hurt herself? Kill herself? Or— God help her—someone else? "I'm scared," she admitted rather reluctantly.

"We'll help you," Nanette confirmed. "I'm not sure how—"

"Well, I'm sure," Tristan declared. "We've first got to figure out who he is, why he's haunting you and what it will take to send him on his way. We haven't dealt with anything like this before, and we'll need help from the other side, especially if this guy is trying to hurt you."

"We can check with Ryan," Jenee said. "He may have some ideas, since he was in the middle for a while. And we could ask Grandma Adeline how to send this ghost on his way. Put a note on the tea service and see if she responds." She crossed the kitchen, withdrew a pad of paper from a drawer and wrote a short note. "There. I'll go put this on the tea service and see what happens."

The Vicknairs received their medium assignments via the silver tea service in the sitting room, and apparently, they had the means to communicate with Adeline Vicknair in the same manner, though Chantelle hadn't seen that occur during her stay at the plantation last fall. Could the Vicknair matriarch, currently residing in the other realm, help Chantelle get rid of her personal specter? She had to admit, it was worth a try.

"How long does it usually take her to respond?" she asked.

"It varies," Nanette said. "Sometimes immediately, and sometimes awhile. We're still learning about how things work when communicating with the other side, but Grandma Adeline has never let us down. And besides, Tristan feels a ghost coming, so he should get something on the tea service soon, anyway. Maybe she'll use that same opportunity to let us know what to do about your ghost."

A small surge of relief inched through Chantelle and made her feel better. She had the Vicknairs, even their grandmother on the other side, willing to help; she wasn't facing this thing on her own.

"In the meantime, you aren't going to be alone," Tristan said, and again, it seemed more like a command than a statement.

Chantelle decided she was sick of his orders, even if she didn't want to be alone. "Who will be with me?"

"Me."

"I don't think—"

He cut her off. "Listen, you're dealing with a male spirit, and apparently a vicious male spirit, at that. I don't think there's anyone here who would deny that you need to be with one of us, in case we can get some help from the other side to make this ghost leave. And since you are dealing with a man, then it only makes sense to have a man help you deal with him."

"You aren't the only male Vicknair," Chantelle pointed out, not because she wanted Dax or Gage to watch over her, but because Tristan was pissing her off and she wanted to return the favor.

"I'm single," he said resolutely. "Therefore, I have more time to help you deal with this."

"I'm not staying with you at your apartment," Chantelle declared, and she meant it. She did believe that they needed to handle this obvious tension between them, and she knew she probably owed him an explanation for leaving him that morning. But there was *no way* she could handle dealing with the ghost and also dealing with all the obvious friction between herself and a ticked-off Tristan Vicknair while the two of them tried to cohabit in his tiny apartment. No way. No how.

"O-kay," Nanette interjected, cutting her eyes at Tristan, then softening her look as she turned her attention to Chantelle. "Even though he sounds like a complete caveman with his demand, I agree with Tristan. But you wouldn't have to stay at his apartment. You could stay here."

"Nan…" he warned.

"And," she continued to Tristan, "you could move back in here while she's dealing with this ghost. You've got a letter coming, anyway. That would put you here when the assignment arrives and it would put you near Chantelle when her ghost makes another unwanted visit. *And* you could help more with the house repairs if you stayed here, too, which would be great, since Roussel is checking our progress on Monday."

"I would stay here," Chantelle said, keeping her eyes on Nanette, instead of Tristan. "But if I'm going to, I'll need to go back to my apartment and get my things, specifically my laptop so I can work."

"Writing another book?" Kayla asked.

"I'm trying a sequel." While her book was doing fairly well regionally and had put enough money in her pocket for her to live on for a while, Chantelle wasn't counting on it to support her long-term. "Kayla, would you drive me to my apartment?"

Kayla didn't get a chance to answer. Tristan abruptly stood and instantly reminded her how intimidating the tallest Vicknair with the incredible fireman's build could be. "Are you sure you're up to riding over there? An hour ago, you were trapped in the middle of an airbag in your car."

"I told you I'm fine," Chantelle said, standing, as well, and hating that her five-foot-six didn't come anywhere near his six-foot frame. "Kayla and I will go get my things, and then—"

"No, *we'll* go get your things," Tristan said. "I told you, you're not going to be alone until we get rid of that ghost."

"Which is why Kayla will take me." Her cheeks stung, and she had no doubt Tristan could see the evidence of her irritation. Could he also sense her attraction? Because in spite of the fact that he was without question an overbearing jerk, she wanted him.

"Chantelle, no offense, but that ghost successfully wrecked your car a little while ago. If he's going to give that another try, I'd much rather my wife not be in the vehicle," Gage said. "And truthfully, you probably shouldn't get back on the road, either. Maybe you could tell us what you want out of your apartment, and we could go pick it up."

"It'd be tough for me to tell you where everything is," Chantelle argued. "I'd really rather get it myself, and I think as long as I'm not the one driving, Kayla and I will be fine."

"Kayla isn't driving you, though," Tristan said. "I am."

When none of the others rose to her defense, Chantelle reluctantly accepted that the only way she was going to get all her things out of her apartment herself was to let Tristan take her, even if it meant being alone with him in a vehicle for more than an hour each way, to and from her apartment.

"Fine."

5

TRISTAN PARKED his Jeep at Chantelle's apartment and followed her to the door. A hint of her perfume, or perhaps her shampoo, drifted behind her, a fruity scent that made him want to step closer. Not that *that* would go over well, since she hadn't said more than a dozen words to him throughout the entire drive, and that was only to tell him where to turn. "Take a right there... Turn left... Third brick building on the right." Each directive was delivered in a clipped, sharp tone, without so much as a glance in his direction. She was annoyed, and he couldn't blame her. He'd been a royal ass.

What had come over him at the plantation, talking to her as though he had the right to tell her what to do and as though she had no choice but to let him play the part of her personal watchdog?

Hell, Tristan knew what had come over him. Fear. But not fear of that damned ghost that was trying to hurt her, but fear of her being hurt by that ghost or by anyone else. He couldn't even describe the emotion that had surged through him when he'd realized Chantelle was the woman in the car speeding toward that shed. He'd never felt so helpless, watching her crash merely feet away, and unable to do a damn thing to stop it.

He couldn't deny that she'd been on his mind constantly since their one night together, and it wasn't solely because she'd left him high and dry the next morning. He cared about her, and more than that, he wanted Chantelle Bedeau to *want* him to care about her. There had been something between them, always, in spite of the way they'd fought on the surface. In fact, he suspected that the conflict between them had been primarily because of the strength of the sexual tension ever present beneath the surface of their relationship and keeping them both on edge. Even if their lovemaking hadn't been anything for the record books, whether Chantelle admitted it or not, they *had* connected emotionally, and he knew they could connect physically, too, if he could figure out what barriers kept her from letting go and help her break them down.

Dammit, he'd let his frustration get the best of him at the plantation, trying to pick a fight with her, instead of letting her know he wanted another chance. He needed to remedy that mistake, right here, right now. "Chantelle," he began to say, following her into the apartment.

She turned, sky-blue eyes intent as she spoke. "I know. I shouldn't have left you like that after we slept together, and I regret it, okay?" She balled her hands into fists and settled them on her hips. The stance pushed her breasts up and forward, causing her pink T-shirt to stretch to contain them. Tristan hoped his natural response to the action wasn't noticeable. She obviously wasn't in the mood to know that her flare of temper was turning him on.

"But I'm *not* going to let you treat me like dirt because of what happened back then," she went on.

"I'd have been *fine* with Kayla driving me here, and I'd have been *fine* staying at the Vicknair plantation without you there, so don't try to make me feel as though I should be grateful to have you *and* your attitude around. I don't deserve it. I asked you to sleep with me, and you did. Thank you." She lifted one shoulder. "You gave me what I asked for. And I can't see why my leaving the next morning should piss you off so much. It wasn't as though we'd been dating or anything. We slept together, and then I left. I thought that was what guys liked, anyway—no strings, no commitment. It shouldn't be such a big deal."

The apology he'd been planning refused to pass through his lips. In fact, Tristan's jaw clenched and his mouth remained closed, because he wasn't sure he could control what would come out if he opened it. She was putting on an act, building her walls again, the same way she'd done that night when she faked those orgasms, and the performance infuriated him now as much as it had then. Or rather, as much as it had the next morning, when he'd put two and two together and realized that she was a damn decent actress—and he'd been played. He wasn't going to be played again, about whether she felt something toward him *or* about the fact that he knew he could make her toes curl. He just needed another chance.

"I'll get my things," she said, turning around so fast that her blond curls swirled like a golden cape behind her, and that scent—apples, he realized—teased his senses again.

But suddenly a more powerful scent took its place. Smoke. And stronger than before. Shit, now he was going to have *two* ghosts to deal with, the one haunting the blond pistol that had just headed to the back of her apartment, and the one summoning him back to the plantation.

He waited for her to return and seriously prayed it wouldn't be long. A faint crackling sound—burning wood—had joined in with the smoke. His ghost was getting closer to making an appearance. "Chantelle, we don't have long," he called, but naturally, he didn't receive a response.

He took advantage of his time by surveying her living room, painted and decorated in earth tones, browns and tans and greens, and noted that everything—everything— was in its place. Orderly was the way he'd describe it, with coffee and end tables polished, candles or lamps neatly centered on each, and tall bookshelves on both sides of an entertainment center with every book lined up per- fectly to the edge, spines flush and titles visible. Tristan stepped closer and realized they were even alphabetized by author. Then he looked toward the kitchen. No small appliances cluttered her counters, merely an assembly of tall, olive-green canisters, lined up like soldiers next to the stove. Unlike his own apartment, there were no pot holders tossed on the counter, no dishes in the sink, not even a speck of dust to be seen on any surface. The only item that seemed out of place was a small, battered clock radio, the kind you usually saw beside the bed, sitting on top of her trashcan with the plug dangling off the side.

He didn't do anything big at first—turned on the television and caused the radio to play "Unchained Melody," even when it wasn't switched on. But I kept feeling like I was being watched, you know?

Hell. After all the arguing about staying with her, he'd let her go to the rear of her apartment alone, where a ghost that had already tried to hurt her once could be waiting for a repeat performance. "Chantelle!" He quickly headed down the hallway, rounded the corner into the last room—and stopped still.

She stood beside her bed wearing nothing but a pair of lacy navy panties, high cut and extremely sexy. The matching bra was in her hand, and she moved it in front of her full breasts at his entrance. The clothes she'd been wearing a few minutes ago, the pink T-shirt and jeans, were on the bed, pink panties and bra tossed on top of them. "Tristan," she said, swallowing hard. "What are you doing?"

"I thought your ghost might have come back, and I didn't want you to be alone." It wasn't at all easy to say, given that his throat was growing tight and his cock was growing hard.

"He isn't here. I would have called for you if I sensed him," she added, still holding the navy fabric against her chest. "And I believe I'll be okay to change clothes on my own, if you don't mind."

"Right." He tried to get his legs to move. She looked so good and he'd wanted her for longer than he cared to admit, but they still had things to work out; he still had things to find out. As had been the case before with Chantelle Bedeau, the timing wasn't right.

He noticed the suitcase and computer bag propped against her bedroom door. "These ready to go?" he asked, attempting to keep himself from sounding the least bit aroused. Not an easy feat.

"Yes." She slid her arms through the bra straps, then

fastened the back closure. One nipple peeked above the lace with the maneuver, and Tristan immediately recalled the way her nipples had turned to hard stiff pearls against his tongue.

Scooping up the two bags, he left the room as though he hadn't seen her nearly naked, hadn't remembered how incredible that curvy body felt against his, hadn't noticed the slight flush to her cheeks when she realized he was in her bedroom and looking at her in her sexy underwear.

Within minutes she joined him in the living room. The pink shirt and jeans had been exchanged with a navy top and khaki shorts, so now Tristan had to control the currently dominant part of his anatomy while looking at smooth tanned legs. The woman was trying to kill him.

"I was hot in the jeans," she said by way of explaining her change of apparel.

"No problem." She was hot *out* of her jeans, too, but he wasn't about to say so.

"You said we don't have long," she reminded him. "Until what? I didn't realize we had a set time to get back." She grabbed the computer bag from where he'd placed it on the couch and started toward the door, ever Ms. Independent.

Tristan would've taken the bag from her, but she never gave him the chance, walking out ahead of him as though nothing at all had just transpired between them in her bedroom. Then again, maybe she hadn't thought a thing about it. But Tristan sure had—a few things, in fact. And a few positions. He noticed how she continued walking, hurriedly, without looking back.

Oh, yeah, she was thinking about those things, and she was trying to leave the sexual pull behind her just as she'd done before. Nice try.

He carried out the suitcase, closed the door and checked the lock, then joined her in the Jeep.

"I asked if we have a certain time to get back." Chantelle still didn't look at him; instead, she turned to check her bags in the back seat.

"I smelled smoke again," he said. "So I thought my ghost was getting ready to show and, therefore, we'd need to get back. But right now, the scent is gone." And he didn't smell anything but her crisp apple shampoo, claiming the tiny space within the Jeep thanks to all those luscious blond curls tumbling wildly down her back and across her shoulders.

"Does that mean your ghost isn't coming?" Finally she looked his way, and he saw that her cheeks were more flushed than they'd been earlier. Embarrassed? Or excited? Either way, she didn't seem irritated with him anymore. On the contrary, she seemed curious— which made sense, given she was an up-and-coming author who happened to write about ghosts in the central realm.

"It *could* mean my ghost isn't coming, but chances are it means that he or she is taking a little longer getting to the middle than the powers that be had thought." He didn't elaborate by telling her that it probably meant the person was going through a slow, perhaps painful death, and their spirit was teetering between the world of the living and the dead. Right now, the spirit could still potentially go either way, but given how often Tristan had smelled smoke, he believed it was merely prolonging the inevitable, trying to hold on to life for a tiny bit longer, perhaps because he or she wanted a little more time with loved ones, or maybe waiting for a certain friend or family member to arrive. Spirits could find amazing strength at times like that, when they wanted a few more precious seconds with someone they cared about, almost like a living person when a surge of adrenaline set in. During those final moments on this side, they didn't take time for granted...

...the way Tristan was taking time for granted now. He was finally with Chantelle and he should do something about it. He had his hand on the key, but didn't turn on the ignition. He'd left the top on his Jeep and the windows were up, since he'd opted for air-conditioning in the heat of the afternoon. Without the car turned on, the interior of the vehicle quickly grew very hot. Steamy. And it wasn't totally due to the lack of air-conditioning. He looked at the woman in the passenger seat, noticed those blue eyes searching his for some hint of his intention.

Her breathing quickened. She ran her upper teeth across her lower lip, and he noticed a slight sheen on her face, her neck, and on the sexy shadow of her cleavage within the V of the navy top. "Tristan, we can go now."

"No, we can't. Not until you tell me."

She moistened her lips, swallowed again, then shifted uncomfortably in her seat. "Tell you what?"

No time like the present. He wanted to know, and the only way to find out was to ask. "Why you faked it that night three times. And more than that, why you left the next morning."

CHANTELLE'S WORLD tilted off center. There were way too many things happening at once, too fast, too intense, and she had sensory overload. The scent of Tristan Vicknair, all male and musk and tempting, filled every breath she took. After nearly six months without seeing him since their night together, he was here, with her, and he'd be with her until her ghost was gone. How long would that be? And how could she keep up her cool facade for the entire duration?

When he'd walked in to her room and seen her in her underwear, she'd tried to act as though it hadn't shaken her to the core—and done other, more tingly things to her core, as well. Everything in her had quivered at the mere sight of him in her bedroom, where she'd had many heated dreams of the two of them and the way they were that night, except in her dreams she didn't hold back. On the contrary, in her dreams, her entire body quaked, and spasms claimed her completely, and she came as though the world were ending, screaming through her release. But then she'd awaken and realized that it was merely a dream. And that even her dreams, as realistic as they were, couldn't get her where she so desperately needed to go.

Tristan leaned across the seat, those green eyes moving in, entrancing her, as did the gorgeous strong face that said he was afraid of nothing—and intent on one thing. "You did, didn't you?" he asked, and the sound of his voice, that same low seductive tone he'd had that night in his apartment, made her wet. "You faked all of them, didn't you, Chantelle?" He moved even closer, to where his lips were almost touching hers, and he ran the back of a finger over her cheek, sending a frisson of sheer pleasure shimmying down her spine. She gasped.

"Didn't you?" he repeated, and her head swam, the desire, the heat of this situation, blurring her vision around the edges.

Was she dreaming now?

"Chantelle," he said, and she realized her eyes had fluttered closed, ready to let this dream run its course. Maybe this would be the one that would give her the release she wanted. It sure seemed real, felt real…

"Tristan," she whispered, her voice urgent, her need urgent.

"Why did you fake it, Chantelle?"

"I…didn't." She could lie in a dream, couldn't she? The Tristan in her dreams would believe her, and then he'd continue doing…everything he was doing that was getting her so incredibly hot.

"Yeah, you did," he said, and she felt the heat of his words against her lips. "But you're not faking this now, are you?" Then his mouth closed over hers, his fingers cradled her face, and he teased her lips apart. His tongue slipped inside, and he tasted as good as he did last time, warm and minty and right, and she moaned her contentment.

He responded by deepening his thorough perusal of her mouth, letting his tongue mate with hers while her body grew hotter and hotter, her hips lifting off the seat in anticipation, in desire, in need. His hand moved to her breast and caressed it through her shirt, and she wished she was naked again, the way she'd been earlier in her bedroom, before he came in.

She squirmed in the seat, her shorts suddenly very

constrictive. She wanted them off. She wanted to be free of clothing, free of inhibition, free of fear…free to let Tristan bring her to a place she'd never known.

Free of fear. The thought whispered through her very being, and another memory invaded the perfection of the moment. As Tristan's hand moved from her breast down her abdomen, Chantelle struggled to keep her mind on *his* mouth kissing her deeply, *his* hand massaging her tenderly, *his* body heating her to boiling.

Be quiet. Stop fighting, dammit. You know this is what you want.

The venom behind those horrid words from her past made her shiver. *No.* It was more than the memory, she realized, as Tristan broke the kiss. The air around her had chilled, and her entire body trembled.

"Chantelle? What's wrong? Tell me."

"Don't you feel him?"

The locks clicked loudly into place, and Tristan's eyes widened as he obviously realized they were no longer alone. He reached across her, grabbed the door handle and yanked it hard. It didn't budge. He cursed, loudly, but Chantelle was so cold, so icy, that she couldn't focus on his words.

Then the Jeep shook, only slightly at first, but she felt it.

"Leave her alone, you bastard!" Tristan slammed his fist against the side of the door at the same time that something powerful hit Chantelle's door and rattled the window. Her ghost was literally shaking the car.

"Tristan!" she screamed, moving toward him.

"I've got you," he said, pulling her closer, then brought his hand to the key. "Hold on." He turned on the ignition, and the Jeep roared to life. But as he slammed it into reverse and backed up, a large rock lifted from the ground and hurtled through the air directly toward the windshield in front of Chantelle.

"Get down!" Tristan yelled, shoving her to the floor just as the glass exploded.

6

"DON'T MOVE!" Tristan yelled over the wind whipping through the hole in the windshield.

Chantelle had no trouble following that instruction and wasn't about to argue with him about it. She was too scared to move, and she wasn't sure what would happen with all of the glass on her if she did. She was covered with it, several of the sharp edges penetrating her shirt and pressing into her skin.

"Do you still feel him?" he asked, again very loudly, driving the Jeep away from her apartment—and her ghost.

"No!" Chantelle shouted as loud as she could, since her head was still ducked toward the floor and she wasn't certain Tristan could hear her over the roar of the engine and the whoosh of the wind.

She didn't feel the ghost anymore, and she believed he'd left. But he would come back, and the thought sent another chill through her bones. He'd tried to hurt her again, maybe even kill her. And he'd seemed so angry. She'd sensed the anger, the cold chilling hatred, and she now was sure there was more to it than a ghost merely frustrated about being between worlds. What had she written in her book that would make a ghost want to kill her?

"He wants to kill me," she said, but Tristan didn't hear.

"I'm pulling over," he said a few moments later. "Stay still a little longer, until I can get the glass off you." He wasn't yelling, but was still loud enough to be heard. "And then we're going to send that damn ghost to the other side, one way or another. He could've killed you."

"I think that was the idea," she said, as the Jeep rolled to a stop and Tristan climbed out. Gravel crunched as he walked around the vehicle, then opened her door.

"Stay still. I brought us to a Dumpster so I can get rid of that glass." Then he started carefully removing the shards from her back. She could feel tiny pinpricks where the edges had penetrated her skin, but nothing more than that. Tristan's fingers tenderly picked each piece from her right shoulder and arm, where most of it seemed to have landed. Her hair had protected her left side, thank God.

One larger shard had punctured her bicep and was deeper than the other slivers. Tristan carefully removed that one while Chantelle watched.

"We're going to need to clean this," he said. There was blood on her arm, but some of it was his, from where he'd grasped the tiny pieces.

"You're bleeding," she said.

"Yeah, well, so are you. And you know the main problem with that?"

"No."

"I don't have any way to make him bleed."

Chantelle smiled at that; she couldn't help it. In a normal situation, if a living man had invaded Tristan

Vicknair's Jeep or thrown a rock through the windshield, she had no doubt that the guy would receive a
Cajun's introduction to his fist, if not more.

"Chantelle, I'm serious. How am I supposed to
protect you from him if I can't see him?" Tristan didn't
wait for her to answer, but gently brushed his palm
down her arm, then guided her up from the floor. "Come
on. I need you to get out so I can try to get the rest of
it." Then he looked at her again. "You don't feel him
now, right?"

"I don't feel him at all." In fact, the only male
presence she sensed right now was the one currently
removing glass from her body, examining her intently
for scratches and scrapes, and taking care of her in the
aftermath of one of the most terrifying moments of her
life. "Thank you for helping me."

He smirked. "Hell, I don't know what good I did.
Sure, he left, but I'm not fool enough to think he isn't
coming back, and before he does, I need a better game
plan." He took her hand and guided her away from the
Jeep. "I'm not sure what we're going to do about the
pieces in your hair," he said, leaving her momentarily
to grab something out of the back of his Jeep, "but
maybe we can use one of these to contain it until we can
get all the glass out." He returned holding a couple of
blue bath towels. "Lean this way," he said, motioning
for her to bend toward him.

"You keep bath towels in your Jeep?" she asked,
leaning the way he'd instructed, so her hair fell away
from her.

"I shower after I work out at the gym and keep the
towels for that."

Chantelle pictured him hot and sweaty after his workout and then stepping boldly and beautifully naked into the shower. The edge of the towel brushed her neck as Tristan wrapped it around her head. Then he eased her upright and continued tucking it in until her hair was completely in a turban. She reached up and touched the side, found it very secure and gawked at him.

"What?" he asked.

"Just wondering where you learned to do that, since I doubt you have to tie up your hair after a shower."

One corner of his mouth crooked. "Monique. She has a hair salon, remember? When she was first starting out, she practiced her towel tying on anyone who would let her."

"You let her?"

"Monique can be extremely persistent." His green eyes flashed as though daring her to tease him. Any other time, she would have, but not today. Not after how he'd protected her when the ghost attacked and how he'd taken care of her afterward. And not when, in spite of the ghostly attack, she still remembered the way it felt a few minutes ago when he'd touched her, kissed her.

"Chantelle."

"Yeah?"

"We're going to talk about *that* later, but right now we need to get out of here."

She didn't need to ask him what he was referring to; obviously he'd just looked at her and known that her thoughts had been on their heated interaction in the Jeep. What would have happened if that ghost hadn't shown?

She blinked. *Nothing* would have happened, because as she remembered the heat of the moment, she also remembered where her thoughts had inadvertently headed. To the first time she was ever touched, and the fear surrounding it. That had ruined the moment with Tristan before the ghost even made an appearance.

"Hey," Tristan said, putting a knuckle beneath her chin and tilting her face toward his. "We *are* going to talk about it, but not here."

She nodded, deciding not to explain that he'd misinterpreted her reaction. "Where are we going?"

"First we'll go to my place and let me get my things for staying at the plantation. We'll leave the Jeep there, and I'll borrow a friend of mine's pickup. Gerry won't mind. He's always got an extra car he's tinkering on, and that pickup will run well enough to get me by till this is fixed. If my Jeep were newer, it'd have shatterproof glass. Obviously this one doesn't." He motioned at where the majority of his window was missing in action. "Anyway, after we swap vehicles and I pick up my things, we'll go back to the plantation and see if we can get my grandmother, or the powers that be, to give us directions for sending that ghost to hell, where I have no doubt he belongs."

Her eyes widened at that, and he continued.

"There's no way this ghost is merely stuck in the middle and looking for the light, Chantelle. If he were, then he'd be assigned to a medium, maybe even one of us, and we'd help him. This ghost doesn't want to be helped. He wants to hurt someone, and that someone happens to be you. I'm thinking that the powers that be won't tell us how to get this one to the light. What we need them to tell us is how to send him to the *other* side." Tristan draped the second blue towel over her seat. "Here. This will hopefully keep any stray bits of glass from cutting you until we can swap vehicles."

She sat in the seat, then saw him frown as he looked at all of the nicks on her shoulder and arm.

He tenderly touched one, wiping a small dab of blood away. "I'll find a way to make him leave if it kills me."

Chantelle prayed this ghost didn't take that literally. Would it kill Tristan? Would it kill her?

He crossed in front of the car, then climbed in the driver's side. "I'm calling Nanette. I want to find out if Grandma Adeline has answered Jenee's question." He pulled his cell phone from his pocket while he cranked up the engine. Within minutes, they were heading back toward LaPlace and Tristan had relayed everything to Nan.

Chantelle could tell from his end of the conversation that while Jenee's note to their grandmother had disappeared from the tea service, no answers had been left in its place, nor had Tristan's next assignment arrived.

"Yeah, Nanette, I told you we'd stay there, and we will, but I've got to stop by my place first."

In spite of the wind billowing through the Jeep, Chantelle still heard Nanette's voice, loud and obviously upset, as she asked her cousin a ton of questions about what had happened and how Chantelle was handling the situation.

Personally Chantelle thought she was handling it pretty well, considering that since she'd awoken this morning, she'd been attacked twice by a ghost. The first time Tristan had been there within seconds, and the next time he was right beside her when the spirit returned. Something about him being there and knowing he would be there whenever the enraged specter made another appearance made her confident that the two of them would send the ghost on his way— as soon as they learned how.

Tristan finished his conversation with Nanette as they pulled up beside the canal that led to his apartment.

"There's Gerry," he said, indicating a guy leaning under the hood of an older-model car. The man stood when he heard the Jeep, and Chantelle noticed he was one of the firemen who'd checked on her after her accident. He still wore the navy fireman's shirt, like the shirt Tristan currently wore and like the shirts that all the firemen had been wearing this morning at the Vicknair house, but he'd exchanged his jeans for gray gym shorts, and his arms were covered in grease. His forehead, and the majority of him, dripped with sweat, and he squinted at them as though some of it had burned his eyes.

"Hell, what happened to your Jeep?" he asked as they climbed out.

"A rock," Tristan said, not elaborating that the rock in question had been tossed by a dead guy. "Gonna send it over to Paul Boudreaux's place to get it fixed, but I'll need something to drive in the meantime. You planning to use the truck anytime soon?"

Gerry shook his head. "Nah, and the keys are in it. Have at it." Then he grinned. "Just watch out for rocks." He cocked his head to the side and looked at Chantelle. "D'you hit your head?"

She touched the towel turban. "No, but I did get some glass in my hair."

"And on your arm, from the look of things," Gerry added, peering toward her pricks and scratches. "I'm guessing you got what you need to clean her up, Chief?"

"Yeah," Tristan replied, leading Chantelle toward his apartment. "Thanks for letting me use the truck."

"No problem." Gerry ducked back under the hood of the car, and Chantelle and Tristan went into Tristan's place.

"I don't think he even realized that you're the same woman from the crash this morning," Tristan said after he closed the door and they were out of Gerry's hearing. "Obviously Gerry's not the best at keen observation."

"Well, I was covered in an airbag and talcum powder," she noted. "And I didn't have this." She pointed to the turban.

"True." He raised his brows. "You're not feeling him now, are you? The ghost?"

"No, I don't feel him at all." Chantelle scanned his apartment to make sure she didn't sense anything out of the ordinary, anything that would indicate her hellion ghost had followed them here. She took in the couch, where a pillow at one end and a tossed afghan at the other said that Tristan had probably fallen asleep watching television at some point. Stacks of magazines—on home improvement, she noticed—were scattered on the floor beside the couch, and a beer bottle sat on top of a napkin at one end of the coffee table.

"I had no idea I'd have company," he said, obviously seeing his place from her perspective. Messy. Extremely messy.

"At least you put a napkin under the bottle," she teased, and he laughed. That laugh was *nice*.

"Surely you noticed the place was a wreck the last time you were here."

"No," she said softly, "I didn't." All she'd noticed was Tristan, and all she'd felt was how much she wanted him. At the time, she'd thought her main desire was to get him to help her conquer her fear of men. However, after months of thinking about him, Chantelle knew better. Her main desire…was him.

"Well, this is pretty much normal," he admitted.

She smiled at the way he half apologized for his lack of housecleaning. Truthfully, she'd have been shocked to find everything in order. His position at the firehouse demanded such strict order and complete control that he'd have to find release somewhere—and he'd obviously found it here, because there was definitely no order whatsoever. Which meant…he was a human being. Just an adorably messy one.

"You laughing at me, Chantelle Bedeau?"

"Just admiring your housekeeping skills," she said, a hint of a giggle escaping before she swallowed it down and added, "You planning to fix it up?" She indicated the home-improvement magazines.

He shot a sidelong glance her way that said he knew she was changing the subject, moving away from the flirtation, then he answered, "Planning to build a house one day, after we get the plantation house back up to par. But for now I just read the magazines to figure out how we can repair the structural damage on the place before Roussel gets the parish bigwigs to agree with him about tearing it down. He's got the restoration committee for the parish coming over on Monday to examine our progress. Thanks to my guys working on it today, we're ahead of schedule. We don't have to be finished, just prove we're headed in the right direction."

"So you're okay for this inspection?"

"I think we'll keep them from agreeing to tear it down for a while. We've put everything we've got into saving it, and I believe the majority of the committee realizes it, even if Charles Roussel doesn't." He grinned. "Probably kills him that he only has one vote."

"That'd be such a tragedy, to tear it down. Not only is it your family's home, but it's vital for spirits to find their way to the other side. It was the place that helped Lillian cross over," she added, remembering her sister and the way Gage, her assigned medium, had helped her find the light.

"We won't let Roussel win. You're right, that place does help send spirits where they need to go. And hopefully it'll help us send yours where he needs to go, too." He started up the stairs that led to his bedroom and she turned toward the couch.

"Oh, no," he said from behind her, and she pivoted to see that he'd stopped, one foot on the first stair. "You're coming with me."

"I'll wait here." True, they needed to confront whatever was going on between them, but she didn't want to be in his bedroom when they did.

"Listen, I don't want to argue with you, so I'm going to tell it like it is. You're *not* going to be alone, at all, ever, until we know for certain that the bastard that threw that rock through my windshield is gone for good."

"I can feel when he's near. It's cold and creepy," she explained, moving a couple of magazines aside and sitting on the couch. The soft black vinyl chilled her legs, and she rubbed her hands down the sides of her thighs to warm them. "So I'll let you know if I feel anything like that," she said dismissively.

He stood his ground. "You're right. You'll let me know, and it'll be easy to do since I'll be right beside you. Now come on, Chantelle. I don't want to argue about it."

"Could've fooled me." She huffed out a breath. He was right and she knew it; she didn't want to be alone with that ghost still after her—but she also didn't want to go up to his bedroom and see the place where they'd been together and where she'd turned tail and run. After faking a few orgasms. She stood and crossed the room. "Go ahead. I'm right behind you."

He moved back against the wall. "No, you go ahead. *I'm* right behind *you*. Besides, you know the way."

She ignored that and held her breath as she reached him on the narrow stairs so she wouldn't blatantly inhale his intoxicating male aroma as she passed. But the temptation was too great, and she practically absorbed the scent of him, leaning closer to him as she went by, then trying to disguise the fact with a pitiful attempt at missing the next step.

He reached out to steady her, his large warm hands catching her at the waist and inadvertently sliding beneath her shirt in the process.

Chantelle's breath caught in her throat, and desire stirred between her thighs.

"And while we're up there," he said, holding her still, "you can answer my question from earlier." When she said nothing, he continued, "About why you let me believe you came, when you didn't." He released her, so that she could climb the rest of the way up the stairs with him behind her.

Again, she said nothing, just walked ahead of him into his bedroom. She needed to think, to breathe. She needed…Tristan.

His black comforter was tossed aside as though he'd just climbed out of bed, and the burgundy sheets were bunched to one side, as well. The comforter covered one pillow, the other was folded in half and nearly flat. She knew that was where Tristan laid his head—on the one that was well-worn and far from perfect. His house seemed to indicate an appreciation for imperfection, almost an affinity for it.

Chantelle was far from perfect.

She swallowed and took her attention from the bed, but didn't want to look at Tristan yet, either. He'd be able to see too much, like the fact that she hadn't wanted to leave his bed that morning. And then he'd want to know why she had.

Could she tell him?

Her eyes rested on the open door leading to his bathroom. "Tristan?"

"Yeah?" He was right behind her, much closer than she'd realized. Oddly his nearness didn't make her uncomfortable this time, but made her feel warm, safe—and something more that she didn't want to analyze now. She really needed a little time to think about what was happening—with her ghost and with Tristan.

"I'd like to try to get the slivers of glass out of my hair. I'm thinking that if I rinsed it really well, maybe they'd come out without me having to use my hands. Can I use your shower?"

"No." His warmth enveloped her as he apparently stepped even closer, his front very near to her back. He wasn't touching her physically, but he was touching her nonetheless. "Not without me."

Unable to control her response to that, she turned, finally faced those vivid green eyes and firmly stated, "No." She could almost see the two of them naked and rubbing completely against each other beneath a hot spray of water, but when he'd touched her in the car, she hadn't been able to follow through. Like last time, she'd almost—almost—blocked out the horrendous memories of her past, but then she'd heard Romero's voice, those disgusting words he'd hiss in her ear when he forced himself on her and cut her with that horrid knife, and she'd remembered the way it felt every night, to lie in her bed at the orphanage and pray with all her heart that he wouldn't come for her, that he wouldn't take her, that he wouldn't—

"Chantelle, stop," Tristan said, moving in front of her and tilting her face so she looked directly into his eyes. "I don't know for certain what you're thinking right now, but I can imagine. And I shouldn't have said it that way. I won't make you do anything you don't want to do—ever—and when I said I'd go with you to the shower, I meant I'd help you get those bits of glass out of your hair. We can do that without even removing your clothes, I swear." He inhaled, held it a beat, then exhaled slowly. "God, Chantelle, I won't hurt you."

She nodded, her throat clenched and a tear slipped free. "I'm sorry."

"No," he said, shaking his head, then easing his thumb to her cheek and rubbing the tear away. "*I'm* sorry. I think I know what's going on with you, and I want to help." Then he cleared his throat and gave her a slight grin. "But just tell me the truth—you were faking it, weren't you?"

He was trying to lighten the mood, ease away her pain, and it'd be easy for her to lie to him, or joke about what happened that night. But Chantelle wasn't going to lie to him. Not anymore. "It wasn't you. I couldn't…I mean, I can't…"

He moved his thumb to her lips. "We'll talk about it later, whenever you're ready. And we'll try again later, if that's what you want." He tilted his head toward the bathroom. "But now, let's just see about getting that mess out of your hair. I've got an idea. Come on."

She followed him into the bathroom and watched as he turned on the water in the tub, holding his hand under the faucet while he adjusted the temperature.

"Okay, this won't be all that easy to pull off, but I think we can handle it." Tristan motioned for her to step closer to the tub. She did, and then he slowly unwrapped the towel from her head and captured her hair in his hand. "Yeah, definitely still glass in there," he said, and Chantelle looked toward his palms, cradling all her curls.

"Cutting you?" she asked, and felt horrible that there didn't seem to be any way around him getting nicked if he was determined to help her.

"Nothing I can't handle." He guided her to stand directly beside the tub. "Now, kneel down and lean your head over."

She did, and Tristan draped her hair into the tub near the running water.

"Stay there. I'm going to use the showerhead to rinse it out."

Chantelle braced her hands on the cool edge of the tub and kept her head bowed over the side. It felt awkward, but even if Tristan had let her take a shower on her own to get the slivers out, there wouldn't have been any way to do it without possibly cutting herself when the pieces came loose. At least this way, the shards would fall into the tub, instead of on her body.

Tristan stood beside her and then she heard him push the lever that directed the water's flow to the showerhead. Within a second, a warm spray hit her neck, and then gradually moved along her head; she watched her hair darken as the water drenched it completely.

She closed her eyes, enjoying the way the warm water trickled along her scalp, massaging her worries away, helping her fears subside. In spite of her odd position, bent over the side of the tub, Chantelle felt strangely relaxed.

Then she realized that Tristan's hands were moving over her scalp, those talented fingers working through her curls to free every sliver of glass.

"Tristan, you shouldn't—"

"I'm okay. I'm working some conditioner through to make certain all of those tiny pieces slide free."

"But I don't want you to cut yourself."

"I'm okay," he repeated. "I'm not doing anything I don't want to do." His fingers then slid behind her ears and gently rubbed her there, and Chantelle closed her eyes again. This felt very nice. Very *right*.

After rinsing her hair thoroughly, he turned off the faucet, then gently squeezed the excess water from her curls. "Hang on. Let me get a towel." He moved across the bathroom, then returned, and used a soft burgundy towel to wrap her head in the same manner he'd wrapped the blue one earlier. Then he helped her stand from the tub and turned her to face him. The warmth of his hands resting on her shoulders penetrated the thin fabric of her shirt, and the warmth of his eyes looking into hers with open desire penetrated her heart.

"Chantelle."

It was suddenly difficult to swallow, to think, to breathe. "Yeah?"

He simply stood there for a moment, looking at her and giving her time to look at him, really look at him, this incredible man about whom she'd thought nonstop for months, and who had touched her both physically and emotionally. She'd tried to give herself to him before, and she'd failed. Yet he seemed to have forgiven her for that.

"I want you."

She held her tears at bay, but her chin trembled. How could she give herself to him, or to anyone, when getting *that* close meant letting the past in? "I know you do, Tristan, and I want—"

He shook his head before she could finish. "I should've known after that night, instead of making my own assumptions about what happened. I thought I'd finally found a woman I couldn't satisfy, and it pissed me off. Not so much at you, but at myself. Hell, I always thought I was pretty good at, well, everything." He grinned.

"Modest, aren't ya?" she said, almost laughing through the words.

"No, I'm not, but I should be."

"Nothing wrong with stating the truth." She was grateful he'd once again lightened the mood. "I'm sure there aren't many women, if any, you couldn't satisfy. If I were a normal—"

"But Chantelle, you *aren't* normal," he said, running a finger along her jaw, then easing it down the column of her neck and sending a shiver of anticipation through her veins. How could a mere touch do so much? But she knew. It wasn't a mere touch—it was Tristan's touch.

"You aren't normal," he repeated. "You're the most unique woman I've ever known, and I think that's what made your leaving me that morning so difficult to swallow. I couldn't stand the fact that I wanted you so much and that I couldn't give you what you needed." He paused, then lowered his voice as he added, "I still want to, Chantelle. But like I said earlier, I don't do anything I don't want to do, and I don't want you doing anything you don't want to do, either."

She didn't want Tristan thinking that any part of what had happened was his fault. It wasn't. It was *her* hang up, and her problem to deal with, if she ever could. "Believe me, it isn't that I don't want you or that you did anything wrong. Everything you did, everything you do, is so right it's scary. And I nearly did, you know, that night."

"You nearly came, you mean," he said, his voice still sexy and low and sending a wave of liquid heat through her.

"I was as close as I've ever gotten to letting go, but—" she decided that the only way for him to understand, really understand, was to know everything "—I can't, Tristan. I can't have an orgasm. I've never been able to at all, because every time I start even thinking about being that close to a man, I remember what happened back then. And I…can't." The tears fell now, and she didn't try to stop them.

Tristan pulled her close, wrapped his arms around her and held her while she cried. His heartbeat pounded steadily against her ear, and his strength surrounded her, shielding her from the past, protecting her from the pain.

"Damn him." His words were barely spoken, but the conviction behind them was palpable. Then he kissed the top of her head. "I'm here, Chantelle. We'll get rid of this lunatic spirit that's trying to hurt you now, and then I swear I'll help you deal with the past and help you have…everything you've ever wanted."

7

GAGE AND KAYLA were exiting the back of the Vicknair plantation house when Tristan parked Gerry's pickup next to Gage's truck.

Kayla rushed to the passenger side and opened Chantelle's door. "Nanette told us what happened. Are you okay?" She gasped when she saw Chantelle's right arm covered in a surplus of small bandages.

"I'm okay," Chantelle said. "Tristan overdid it a bit on the doctoring. It isn't as bad as it looks." In fact, he'd taken extreme care to make certain no cut, nick or scrape went unattended. He'd also taken extreme care to brush and blow-dry her hair, telling her he didn't want her to aggravate the cuts by lifting her arm.

She would never have imagined that the simple act of blow-drying could be so sensual. She'd sat in a chair in his bathroom, much like she'd sit in a stylist's chair at a beauty salon, while Tristan stood behind her. He'd gently brushed her hair as he dried it, guiding the soft bristles of the hairbrush over her scalp and down the length of her curls. Chantelle had closed her eyes and simply enjoyed the feeling of having a man—of having Tristan Vicknair—truly care for her. She'd felt no fear then; each time his body had brushed against hers as he moved around her in the small space, she'd simply wanted *more*.

"Do you want me to take a look?" Gage's question brought her attention to the present and to Tristan's doctor cousin, his brows dipping downward as he peered at Chantelle's arm.

"I took care of it," Tristan said, gently touching her as he spoke. "She's nicked up pretty bad, but she'll be okay, as long as we can stop the bastard from getting to her again. Any sign of a letter?" He sounded nearly as anxious to learn more about her ghost as Chantelle did.

"Not the last time we checked the tea service," Kayla answered. "Jenee's been going in there every few minutes or so to look, but nothing yet."

"That's Gerry's pickup, isn't it?" Gage asked.

"Yeah. Looks like between Chantelle and me, we're going to give Paul Boudreaux all the business he needs this weekend."

"I can't believe a ghost attacked you," Kayla said to Chantelle. "And you still don't have any idea who it is?"

"No, I don't. But I do know one thing—he's one mad ghost." She attempted to make it sound as though it didn't scare her out of her wits that this crazed spirit had zeroed in on her.

Kayla wasn't fooled. "Do you want me to stay here tonight? Gage and I could spend the night here so I could be with you in case he comes back."

"Thanks, but I'll be okay. Tristan is going to help me deal with him." She said the words casually, but knowing he would be with her, helping her battle the ghost, as well as the demons of her past, touched her more than she could express.

Kayla nodded. "I'm glad." Chantelle knew Kayla well enough to realize that the two words meant more than she was glad Tristan would help her friend deal with the ghost. She was glad Tristan was going to be with Chantelle, period. And truthfully Chantelle was, too.

I swear I'll help you deal with the past and help you have…everything you've ever wanted.

What she wanted right now, more than anything else, was the man talking with Gage. The two of them had stepped away from the truck and were speaking so low that she couldn't hear what was said, but she could tell by the intensity on Tristan's face that he was conveying the magnitude of her ghost's attack.

"Chantelle?"

She turned back to her friend. "Yeah?"

"Let him," Kayla whispered. "Let Tristan help you." She glanced toward Tristan and Gage to make sure they weren't listening; they weren't, too deep in their own discussion to notice that Chantelle and Kayla were talking low, as well. "I noticed it after Lillian died. Tristan, trying to get you to open up to him, to get closer to you, and you, shutting him out. And the fact that you asked him to sleep with you to help you overcome the past says that you already trust him more than any other man."

Chantelle's chest tightened, her emotions gripping her heart. "But I know I hurt him when I left. I don't want to do that to him again—let him give me everything and give him nothing in return. What if I'm never able to truly be intimate with any man?"

Kayla's lower lip rolled inward for a moment before she finally spoke. "It took me some time to trust Gage, too. That's just part of our dealing with our past." She stepped closer. "It's Romero, isn't it? He's still messing with your head, even though he's dead."

Chantelle nodded. In fact, there were two Romeros who'd abused them back then, but the women hadn't realized until last year that the son was also involved in the abuse. Kayla was referring to Wayne, the father, who had been murdered in prison. The son, A. D. Romero, was still alive, but thank God, behind bars.

"I know what it's like to try to get past it," Kayla said. "At times it seems almost impossible, like no matter how hard you want to let someone else in, to willingly give your body to the man you care about, you just can't, because the past is always there. It's a part of you, a part of us—the abuse, the trial, Lillian's murder, all of it. But you *can't* let the past control your future." She frowned slightly. "I mean, you can, but you shouldn't. Tristan obviously cares about you, the way Gage cares about me, enough to understand. I can see it when he looks at you, and I can tell you feel the same way when you look at him."

"I do care about him," Chantelle admitted. "But every time we get close enough that I could really lose myself in him, really let myself go…"

"You think of what happened to you back then."

She nodded. "But Tristan said he's going to help me, not only with the ghost, but also to face the past."

Kayla's smile claimed her face. "And like I said— let him."

Gage and Tristan had stopped talking, and they walked toward Chantelle and Kayla.

"You ready to head home?" Gage asked, wrapping an arm around Kayla and kissing her cheek.

"Sure." She looked toward Chantelle. "We were thinking about driving back over here later tonight to eat—Nanette and Jenee are cooking enough jambalaya for an army—but I think we may just stay in and rent a movie. I'm really tired for some reason."

Gage hugged her. "You're really tired from working on this house all afternoon."

"I guess you're right," Kayla said, leaning into him. "So it's okay with you to lay low at the apartment tonight, instead of coming back here to eat?"

"Sounds great. And besides, most of that food they're cooking is going over to the firehouse, anyway." He grinned at Tristan. "You can't beat the rate for your fire guys. They gave us a full Saturday's work, again, and damn near have this place ready for Roussel's inspection Monday, and all we have to do is feed them."

"I forgot that food's being sent over there," Kayla said. "Guess you two better make sure you get a plate before they leave with it, huh?"

"We should." Tristan looked toward the house. "But before I grab a plate of anything, I'd better see what Grandma Adeline has for my next assignment."

"It's here?" Chantelle asked. He'd asked Gage about the letter just a moment ago, yet now he sounded as if the letter's arrival was a fact.

"I'll be surprised if it isn't," he said, inhaling thickly, his face tense. "Not only can I smell smoke, but I feel the fire, hear it popping and crackling. Yeah, I've got a letter inside. Let me grab our bags and then we should get to the sitting room."

As soon as he spoke, Chantelle spotted Jenee leaning out the back door, her long brown hair shining brilliantly as it caught the last glints of afternoon sunlight. "Tristan!" she yelled. "It's here!"

"I'll take your things in before we go," Gage said, moving toward Gerry's truck and withdrawing Chantelle's suitcase and computer.

Kayla grabbed Tristan's duffel. "Yeah, we'll take these in. You go get that letter." It never ceased to amaze Chantelle how every member of the Vicknair family understood that their ghostly assignments took priority over everything else, and bonded together to help each other as though every assignment from the other side was his or her own. She wondered how that would feel, having an entire group of people you could count on, know that they cared as much about you as they did for themselves. She caught Tristan's gaze and could've sworn he looked at her as though telling her that she already had someone who cared that much.

"Thanks," he said to Gage and Kayla, then took Chantelle's hand as though it were the most natural thing in the world to do. Chantelle didn't protest; she didn't want to. In fact, letting him have the control he craved, even in as small a matter as letting him take her hand, felt comforting. Reassuring. Not because she was letting a man take control, but because she was letting *Tristan*.

By the time they passed through the mudroom to the kitchen, he'd started coughing, and sweat beaded his forehead.

"Thank goodness you're here," Nanette said. She stood at the stove stirring the jambalaya base in a huge cast-iron pot. The seasonings were strong, tickling the back of Chantelle's throat as she inhaled, but she knew that wasn't what made Tristan cough so violently. He ac-

knowledged Nanette with a jerky nod, then continued
through the kitchen, still clasping Chantelle's hand, in
spite of the discomfort his ghost's arrival was causing
him.

"Oh, man, this one's strong, isn't it?" Jenee asked as
Tristan and Chantelle passed her in the hall before
starting up the stairs toward the sitting room.

Tristan didn't answer as he climbed the stairs with
Chantelle by his side. He burst through the doors
leading to Adeline Vicknair's infamous sitting room.

"Are you okay?" she asked, noticing his hair was
suddenly damp with perspiration, as though he'd just
finished a rigorous workout, instead of merely climbing
a few stairs.

He nodded, then practically fell onto the settee that
occupied the center of the room.

Red and burgundy and pink cloaked the sitting room
completely, from the blinding red velvet on the settee
to the pink floral wallpaper covering every wall to the
heavy burgundy fabric that draped both windows. Everything in the room was feminine, even the lavender
letter on the tea service.

Eyes squinted as though filled with smoke, Tristan
reached for the envelope that contained his next ghostly
assignment.

Jenee had followed them into the room, and she and
Chantelle watched silently as his skin seemed to instantly cool, his cough immediately stopped, and relief
visibly washed over him as soon as he touched the pale-
purple letter that had traversed the boundary between
the living and the dead. Adeline Vicknair's summons to
her oldest grandson.

"Ryan came by earlier, and we asked him if he'd ever encountered evil spirits when he was in the middle," Jenee said. "He hadn't."

Tristan nodded as though he'd expected that.

"Anyway, you're okay now?" she asked from her position near the door.

"Yeah, I'm okay now."

"Then I'm going back to the kitchen to help Nanette. We're supposed to deliver the food to the firehouse in a half hour, and we're running behind. Let us know if you need any help with your assignment, and let us know how we can help you with Chantelle's ghost too, if you find out anything from that letter."

"I will. Thanks, sis." He still appeared to have some trouble speaking, as if his throat was still recovering from smoke inhalation.

"You going to stay with Tristan, or do you want to come to the kitchen and hang out with us?" Jenee asked Chantelle.

"She's staying with me," Tristan said, and Chantelle nodded. No way was she leaving now, not when that letter might tell her how to send her malevolent ghost on his way. She moved to sit beside Tristan on the settee while Jenee headed back downstairs.

Chantelle would have wanted to stay, anyway, regardless of whether the letter told her more about her ghost. Even though she'd spent time at the Vicknair plantation last fall, she'd never seen an actual assignment arrive on the tea service, and she certainly never saw one of the Vicknair mediums go through what Tristan had just experienced, a nearly painful summons from his grandmother on the other side. He'd honestly looked like he was walking through a blistering fire to get to that letter, but strangely enough, he now looked completely at peace and ready to do his job.

Chantelle tried to imprint every aspect of the experience on her memory. This was exactly the type of thing she'd tried to depict in her novel, but her imaginings couldn't compare to the real thing. It was amazing, what he'd do for spirits that he didn't even know. And she knew that with Tristan, it went beyond his duties as a medium. It was the same conviction that had him saving people in fires; the same conviction he'd shown in helping her.

"You sure it's okay for me to stay with you while you read your assignment?" she asked.

Tristan cleared his throat, swallowed and then spoke with a voice that sounded closer to normal. "If it weren't, she'd let us know." He tapped the envelope with a wink.

That wink was probably meant to be cute, but it surpassed cute by a long shot and hit the sexy mark, and Chantelle suddenly had the urge to kiss his eyes and feel those long dark lashes against her lips. She'd do that sometime soon. And hopefully, if she could just "let him" as Kayla had instructed, she'd do more.

Tristan was still looking at the letter, so he hadn't noticed that Chantelle's attention had moved from the intriguing envelope to the equally intriguing man holding it. "I'd love to say I can control what happens in this room, but if Grandma Adeline didn't want you in here, believe me, you wouldn't be here. In this room, she rules. She did when she was living, and that didn't change when she stopped breathing. I guess you saw how determined she can be when she wants something. If I hadn't been just outside the plantation when this arrived and had to deal with that internal fire while trying to drive over here, well, let's just say it wouldn't have been easy."

"I'd have driven you."

He touched her cheek, and Chantelle turned her face toward his fingers, relishing the intimate gesture.

Let him.

He smiled. "I'm sure you would have this time, but believe me, there've been plenty of times I've received assignments when I haven't been anywhere near the plantation and haven't had anyone to drive me. But I deal with it, and I get here. Hell, I'd hate to see what the powers that be would do if I didn't."

"But you'd come, anyway, even if you weren't burning, wouldn't you?" She knew the answer. Tristan wouldn't stay away if he knew a spirit needed his help any more than he would stay away if *she* needed him.

"Yeah, I would."

"I was surprised to see how quickly that letter affected you, and how strongly. Your grandmother is pretty persistent, isn't she?"

"Ask Monique. She's the one who used to fight Grandma Adeline's summonses. I've seen that girl in some serious pain when she had a letter waiting but took her sweet time getting here." He grinned. "I think she understands the seriousness of our obligation now that she's married to a former spirit. Guess she's grateful to them for letting Ryan have another chance on this side, so now she shows up when she's called." He withdrew a pocket knife from his jeans and pulled it across the top of the envelope.

Chantelle flinched, and her blood instantly chilled. She couldn't help it. She hadn't expected him to carry a knife.

Tristan apparently noticed where her gaze had landed, and he snapped the blade closed. "Chantelle, what's wrong? You're white as a sheet. Do you feel him? Is he here?"

"No." She knew she was, as he said, white as a sheet—she'd felt the blood drain from her face—but there was nothing she could do about it. "I…still have a problem with knives of any kind. I guess I always will. He held one against my throat, and if I moved at all, he'd…he'd…" She was dismayed that a tiny muscle in her left cheek twitched involuntarily from sheer terror. Even though it'd been almost ten years, she couldn't control her fear. She still had the tiny spots of discolored skin on her throat, constant reminders of what Wayne Romero's knife had done back then.

Tristan's jaw clenched fiercely, and his eyes smoldered, but not because of his ghost. "Damn him. Damn them both to hell." She knew he meant both Romeros, father and son.

He reached toward the center of the coffee table, jerked a small drawer open and dropped the knife inside. Then he closed the drawer and turned toward her. "I had no idea or I'd have left it at home. Chantelle, tell me what to do. How can I help you?"

"You are helping, more than you realize, just by being with me and by letting me be with you. And I do feel better with it out of sight." She managed to smile. "I'm usually okay as long as I stay away from them, though it does make cooking difficult, let me tell you," she said, and this time her smile came a little more easily. Everything, even her past, seemed easier to handle when she was with him, near him. She nodded toward the envelope. "I think you better handle your assignment, or your grandmother might get upset. I'm betting you don't want to upset her, seeing how merely the appearance of that envelope put you in pain."

He seemed to sense her intense need to move the topic away from the past and the Romeros. "You're right. I wouldn't want you to experience Adeline Vicknair when she's pissed off.

Something slammed against the side of the house, and Chantelle jumped. "What was that?"

He smirked. "A loose shutter hitting the house. It's Grandma Adeline's way of telling me to, one, watch my language, and, two, read the letter."

Evidently deciding he didn't want to further irritate his deceased grandmother, he withdrew several sheets of paper from the envelope; three sheets, she noticed, as he thumbed through them. Her attention honed in on his fingers, long and tanned, a very masculine contrast to the pastel paper. While he read the first page of his assignment, she studied everything else that was so beautifully masculine about the man: strong corded neck, biceps pushing against the short sleeves of his navy T-shirt, broad chest, muscled abdomen. He really was a tribute to his Cajun ancestry.

One finger followed the text on the first page, and Chantelle returned her gaze to that finger, recalling the tender way he'd touched her face earlier, and then the way his hand had cupped her breast.

Her pulse quickened.

"He needs to see his wife once more, make sure

she's okay and say goodbye," Tristan said, turning toward Chantelle as he spoke, then raised his brows. "You weren't reading this, were you?"

"No."

"You're okay?" He looked so concerned, as if he wanted to help her but couldn't fathom how.

"Not yet," she admitted honestly. "But I'm beginning to believe I will be."

"Do you want to read it? If you do, you probably should go ahead, since it won't stay on this side long."

That got her attention. "The letter disappears?"

"You'll see." He placed the sheet in her hand, brushing his fingertips against her palm as he did.

Chantelle was intrigued. "I should have included that in my book," she said, while he scanned the next page.

"I thought your book was fine as it was. I liked the way the ghost always seemed to appear when the couple was on the verge of getting intimate. Reminded me of Monique. She swore Grandma Adeline was trying to keep her from having sex."

Chantelle was taken aback. "You read my book?"

"You wrote it. There was no way I wasn't going to read it and try to learn more about you through your writing."

"It was fiction."

"Uh-huh, and in your fiction, something always kept Evan and Lorelei from having sex, typically something she needed to do to cross over. And in real life, something keeps you from having the same thing."

"Might I remind you that we *had* sex?"

"Yeah, we did, but you didn't come."

"And that's how you knew I didn't come?" she added, realization dawning. Her book had given her away?

"I'd suspected, but yeah, that's how I knew," he said, then leaned toward her and brushed a whisper-soft kiss across her lips. "For the record, I'm determined to help you get rid of that obstacle, and I'm looking forward to the time you finally get to experience what it's all about—with me." He visibly swallowed, then spoke gently. "I know you may never forget the pain of your past, but I want to be the one who helps you see the way it *should* be."

"I want that, too," she said. She did want to experience that with him; it had been the motivation behind her finally asking him to sleep with her after Dax's wedding, and it was the reason that her heart skittered in her chest now. She knew what it was like to want a man, because she wanted Tristan. She just didn't know what it was like to experience true sexual pleasure with that man—yet.

They sat in silence for a moment, and then Chantelle's fingers tingled, and she glanced down in time to see the lavender sheet of paper fade away.

"I didn't get to read it," she said, and he laughed.

"Sorry, Granny," he apologized to the ceiling. "We'll get back on track." Then to Chantelle, he said, "Don't worry. I read it, and that's what matters to her and to my assigned spirit." He handed her the second sheet, and she scanned it quickly, afraid if she didn't that it would also disappear. This page listed the rules for dealing with spirits, basically telling Tristan that he shouldn't waste time, that he couldn't touch a spirit and that he should never abuse the natural bond that occurs between mediums and spirits. As soon as Chantelle finished reading, the page disappeared.

Tristan read the last page and summarized its information for Chantelle. "There's nothing here about your ghost," he said gravely. "She has to know we need help getting rid of him. Or at least some instruction on how to do it."

"You've never had a *bad* ghost before?"

"No, none of us have, but I suspected they existed." One corner of his mouth lifted as he added, "Too many works of fiction describing them for me not to believe that they're true."

"I'm going to have to watch what I put in my books."

"The only reason I read more into your novel is because we'd slept together, and I already suspected the truth."

Chantelle didn't have to worry about any other man reading more into it, then, since Tristan was the only man she'd ever willingly had sex with, and the only man she wanted to have sex with again.

The shutter hit the house with a loud *smack*, and Tristan muttered, "She's getting antsy." Then he called to the ceiling, "You could've helped us with our current ghostly problem, too, you know."

"Maybe you have to take care of your ghost before she can give you information about mine."

He breathed in slowly, his chest pushing against his shirt with the action. "Maybe."

"What does it say about your ghost?" she asked, leaning closer to view the page, and because she simply wanted to be closer to Tristan Vicknair.

"His name is Jake Laberdie, and he and his wife

were in their home in Gramercy two nights ago when the place caught on fire. It was an older home, and I believe it was faulty wiring that started it, though the investigators are still looking into specifics. Anyway, Jake made it out, but then realized his wife was still inside and went back in. He searched and searched, but never found her."

Chantelle looked up from the paper. "How do you know?"

"I know because the letter that you were holding a moment ago told me, and I also know because I found her, Jake's wife."

"You were there?"

Tristan nodded. "We were called to the fire. I found Caroline Laberdie near the back door of the house. She'd passed out from smoke inhalation. She's in the hospital, but she's going to be okay."

"But he didn't make it out?"

"Not on his own. He wasn't coming out without her. We did get him out, but he was in bad shape."

"Did you know that he was the spirit you were getting?" she asked as the final page of his assignment disappeared.

"I suspected, but I didn't know," Tristan said, speaking to Chantelle, but looking toward the window. "Hello, Jake."

8

JAKE LABERDIE wasn't tall, around five-nine at most, but he was as substantial as any wrestler Tristan had ever seen, broad and sturdy, with hair as black as night and eyes the same. Then again, every ghost had black eyes, regardless of what color they'd been when the spirit was living. And like every other ghost Tristan had helped, a golden glow illuminated Jake's body, seeming to emphasize his determination.

He had appeared near one of the sitting room's elongated windows. Tristan recognized him immediately, though he looked nothing at all like he did the last time Tristan had seen him, when over ninety percent of his body had been burned. His face had been practically the only thing unscathed, and that face looked eagerly at Tristan now.

Tristan didn't like knowing that this man had died so young, merely thirty-five, or that he'd left his wife behind; nonetheless, it did make him feel better to see the man's body as it should be, rather than severely burned.

As soon as Tristan acknowledged the ghost, Chantelle had stiffened. He wondered if his interaction with a spirit while she was in the room might frighten her, given her last ghostly encounter, so he reached for her hand and gave it a reassuring squeeze.

Chantelle returned the squeeze and offered him the slightest smile, letting him know that she was okay. He was immensely grateful that she was. He didn't want to ask her to stay if she was uncomfortable, but he also didn't want to let her out of his sight. Not until he knew that her own specter wouldn't come after her.

"I'm looking for Tristan Vicknair," Jake said.

"I'm Tristan and this is Chantelle."

"Adeline said you can tell me how to get to Caroline."

Tristan nodded. "If you can picture her, then you can go to her. And you are due to cross as soon as you spend time with her. According to the information I was given, you can stay with her two days, then you'll cross over."

Chantelle gave his hand another squeeze as she looked toward Jake, still standing by the window. Tristan knew she couldn't see Jake's spirit, but she could obviously tell where he was by watching Tristan. Jake wasn't looking at either of them, though; he'd turned to stare out the window, presumably using his ghostly vision to see his wife in her hospital bed.

"Is she going to make it? Tell me she'll make it," he said, placing his glowing hand flat against the glass of the window as he gazed longingly at his wife.

"Yes, the doctors say she is going to be fine," Tristan affirmed.

"Thank God." Jake's back shook slightly, and Tristan assumed that he was either trembling with relief or crying. "Oh, thank God."

The ghost looked at Tristan again, and no tears were visible. But the sorrow on Jake's face at seeing his wife in that hospital bed, or perhaps at leaving her and having to wait for her on the other side, was palpable.

"What do I do if she can't sense me? Adeline said she'll know that I'm there, but if she doesn't, or if something else goes wrong—" he looked back out the window "—what do I do?"

"If you need me, I'll know," Tristan reassured him. "Just think of me, or of whatever you need from me, and I'll do my best."

"Good, then," Jake said, apparently deciding that if he could see her again and let her know that he was there, even if only for a short time, then he could accept the fact that he was in the middle…and his Caroline wasn't. "So I can go to her now?"

Tristan nodded, and Jake stepped toward the window, his foot disappearing with the action, as though passing through an invisible doorway leading to his wife's hospital room. But then he stopped and jerked around toward Tristan.

"I nearly forgot. Adeline needed me to tell you something about her ghost." He pointed to Chantelle.

Tristan's entire body went on red alert. Grandma Adeline was going to help him, after all. "What about Chantelle's ghost?"

"*She* is the one who makes him stronger. His power over her is directly linked to her fears, all her fears. And the only way she'll ever be rid of him is for her to conquer those fears, *all* of them." Jake glanced toward Chantelle, squeezing Tristan's hand in a death grip now.

"What's he saying about my ghost?" she asked. "Tristan, tell me."

Jake looked at Chantelle and frowned. "Adeline said it's up to you, Tristan, to give her the strength she needs to overcome her fears. And if you can't…"

"If I can't?" Tristan asked, his heart racing.

"He's going to kill her, too."

"What do you mean, 'too'?"

"That's all Adeline said." One corner of Jake's mouth dipped down as he glanced at Chantelle, still gripping Tristan's hand as though her life depended on it.

And maybe it did.

"Tristan, tell me what he's saying, please."

"I'm going to Caroline now, but you need to take care of her. He's watching her now, I can feel him. He's evil. But he can only get to her when her fear lets him." Jake turned, stepped toward the window and disappeared.

"Tristan?" Chantelle looked at him with those crystal-blue eyes, and he could see her concern, her fear.

He can only get to her when her fear lets him.

"What did he say about my ghost? Does he know who it is? Or how we get rid of him?" she demanded. "Tell me what he said." Her hand still held Tristan's, and she placed her other hand on top of his, emphasizing her request. "Please, Tristan. I need to know."

"He didn't know who it is, only that he's evil and that you're the only one who can make him leave."

"How can I make him leave if I can't even see him or know what made him pick me to haunt?"

"Chantelle, he feeds off your fear. That's what makes him strong enough to hurt you."

She released his hand from her grasp, leaned back against the settee and looked straight ahead, at the window where Jake had been merely seconds ago. "He only comes when I'm afraid, and the more afraid I am, the more powerful he is," she said, not really to Tristan, but to herself. "*I'm* making him strong, because I can't get over the past."

"Chantelle, there's something else."

"What?"

"I don't know whether it happened when he was living or whether he can do this after he's dead, but at some point, this person has killed someone. And based on what Jake said and what my grandmother wanted us to know, if I can't help you conquer your fears…"

"He's going to kill me."

9

CHANTELLE SAT at the ancient mahogany table in the Vicknair kitchen and recalled another time she'd been at this table—right after Lillian's murder. Lillian's spirit had been with her then, holding her, comforting her, as Chantelle had mourned her loss. She still missed Lillian severely. There was nothing she'd like more right now than to tell her about the horrible ghost haunting her and trying to hurt her—kill her—and seek that sisterly advice she'd always relied on when they were growing up.

But as much as she wanted to see Lillian again, she didn't want to die for it. She wasn't about to let a madman, or mad ghost, as the case may be, send her to the other side.

Tristan grabbed a pen and paper from the kitchen counter and sat beside her, his face intense. He'd brought her here so they could brainstorm, an activity that often took place in this kitchen, where the Vicknairs planned how they were going to help spirits cross. They'd done that last year, when they were trying to figure out how to help Lillian, but this time it wasn't the whole family; Jenee and Nanette had already left to take the jambalaya to the firehouse, and everyone else had returned to their homes for the night. So she and

Tristan were the only ones here, which made sense. Based on what Tristan had conveyed from Jake Laberdie's instructions, it was up to the two of them to get rid of Chantelle's ghost—before he got rid of her.

"I'm not ready to die," she said. "And I'm not about to let some crazy ghost send me to the other side yet."

His mouth crooked up at one side and his eyes gleamed with approval. "Which is why we're going to do everything we need to do to send him on his way. Starting right now."

"What are we going to do?"

He slid the pen and paper in front of her, nodding to the blank page. "First of all, there's nothing wrong with being afraid of things. I know enough about you to know that you've been battling fear for much of your life, and that isn't your fault—it's Wayne and A. D. Romero's. But this ghost is capitalizing on the fear they created, and no matter how hard you try, you can't fight it on your own." He leaned toward her and tenderly pushed a wayward curl out of her face, then pointed to the paper, still blank.

"What are we doing?"

"Identifying those fears, the ones you've been denying for so long. And then, once we've determined what they are, we'll work on eliminating them completely. All of them. And in the process, we'll eliminate that damned ghost before he hurts you again."

"You mean before he tries to kill me again."

"That's not going to happen. I won't let him, Chantelle, believe me."

She heard the conviction behind the statement and knew that Tristan Vicknair wouldn't let that crazed spirit harm her in any way—if he could stop him. "I believe you." She did, but how was Tristan going to help her conquer all her fears? She'd been fighting them for years and hadn't made any progress. Then again, she hadn't had a ghost trying to kill her if she didn't, and she hadn't had Tristan to help her, either.

He reached for the pen, then wrote two words on the page.

Chantelle read the words, the beginning of her list of fears, and hated that she had so many to conquer. Right now, there were only two on the paper.

Knives

Intimacy

"A nice way to say that," she said, taking the pen from him and tapping the second word.

"I started to write orgasms, but I don't think it's the actual orgasm you're afraid of, is it?"

She expected Tristan to smile, but he didn't. He was honestly asking her if she was afraid to have an orgasm. She didn't want him to have any misconceptions about that. "I've wanted one for as long as I can remember."

He dropped the pen. "You haven't had one, at all?"

Her cheeks burned, but she wouldn't deny the truth. He'd known she hadn't gotten there with him, but what he didn't know was that her body appeared incapable of achieving one at all. "I'd love to tell you that I could at least get there on my own, but I can't. I'm fairly certain I know what it *should* feel like, though, because I think I've been very close."

"When?" he interrupted, his voice dropping with the single word.

She knew he was aware of the answer. Surely he'd felt

how much she was into their lovemaking that night. Her body had burned all over, tingling from his touch, his words, *everything,* and she'd sensed that building spiral of tension, claiming her body, yearning to find release….

"You know when," she finally said.

"You *were* close, weren't you?"

"Closer than I've ever been "

"Then at least I know how to get you close. I just need to work on pushing you on over that edge." He smiled. "I've always liked a challenge."

"But, Tristan, it isn't you. I'd never wanted anyone or anything as much as I wanted to let go completely—with you. But I couldn't." Chantelle shook her head. "How will I this time? And how will I get rid of him if I can't?"

"You can, and you will."

"You've got some kind of new trick to try?" she asked. "Something new in your give-a-girl-an-orgasm arsenal?"

He laughed at that. "I wouldn't say I have an arsenal of tricks for giving orgasms."

"I would," she disagreed, and was thanked by the broad grin that claimed his gorgeous face. Have mercy, merely looking at Tristan had her heart racing.

"I'll take that as a compliment, but I have something much more important on my side this time."

"What's that?"

"I'll know if you fake it. I've seen your incredible acting skills, remember?"

"I said I was sorry about that," she said, guilt making her wince.

"That's not what I mean." He focused on her mouth as he spoke. "What I mean is, I'll know when it's not real, and I'll know when it is. And I promise you, I won't stop until you achieve the real thing, and I don't plan for you to achieve it merely once."

"Trust me, if I figure out how to get there, I sure don't plan to stop at one. In fact, if you can get me there, I'll probably wear you out making you get me there again and again and again."

"I could totally handle you wearing me out," he said, his voice husky and low. Then he looked at the paper and his face sobered. "But I don't think we've listed everything, have we?"

She shook her head and picked up the pen. Before she had a chance to change her mind, she added another line.

Being alone.

"I've forced myself to live alone so that I can try to be independent, in spite of that particular fear," she admitted. "But the truth is, I chose my previous house because the neighbors were all so close, everyone knew everyone and kept up with everybody's business. I liked that. Then, after A.D. attacked Kayla there, I moved to the apartment I'm in now. But again, I picked it because it's in a complex primarily filled with the elderly, and they all love taking care of me, watching over me. I've never really been alone. And I don't want to be."

Tristan looked at the list, a short one—but there wasn't an item on it that would be easy to accomplish, and they both knew it. "Anything else?"

Chantelle thought of one more thing, but she didn't want to add it, didn't even want to admit it. How could she tell him that her ultimate fear was love? That every person she'd ever truly loved had been taken from her and that she didn't think her fragile heart would ever be ready to love again? She shook her head. "No."

He exhaled thickly. "Oddly enough, the toughest one on your list is the last one."

"That I'm afraid of being alone?"

"Yeah, because leaving you alone isn't something that I plan to do, not while that ghost is around."

"But in order for me to conquer that fear, won't you have to?"

"I don't know. That *seems* to be the only way, but like I said, that isn't something I plan to do. I'll talk to the others and see what they think." He was referring to the other Vicknair mediums. "But that's definitely not the one we'll tackle first."

That left knives and intimacy. Chantelle assumed they'd start working on intimacy later, when they were somewhere other than the kitchen. But since they were here now, she reasoned that the best thing to try to conquer first was the only other item on the list. She glanced toward a cutting board, sitting on the counter by the sink, and at the wooden knife block nearby.

"Chantelle, are you sure you're ready for that?" he asked, obviously noticing where her attention had landed.

"The only way to conquer my fears is to face them. I want to, Tristan. I have to or he'll kill me." She gathered her courage. "Help me face this one now."

Tristan looked apprehensive, but he nodded. "Okay, since Nanette and Jenee apparently took all of the jambalaya to the firehouse, we could cook some boudin for sandwiches. And it would need to be cut before we put it in the pan."

"The sooner I conquer my fears, the sooner he

leaves, right?" she stated, but her palms were already starting to sweat at the thought of getting near those knives, much less touching one.

"According to Grandma Adeline, that's the way it works." He stood, moved to the refrigerator and withdrew a package of boudin. "I'm not about to let you try to do this alone, though. And I'm thinking we should take each of the things on your list in stages, a little at a time."

She silently wondered how many stages intimacy would involve and suspected that she'd enjoy each and every one of them. Not as much as she hoped to enjoy the end, if and when she ever experienced an honest-to-goodness orgasm, but the journey to the goal was going to be mighty nice.

Tristan opened the package of sausage and placed the links on the board. Then he paused and tilted his head. "I'm going to have to teach you to play poker sometime."

"Poker?" Where had that come from?

"Yeah, because you need to work on your poker face. I can tell everything you're thinking pretty much all the time, and right now, oddly enough, you're thinking about sex."

"I'm thinking about the steps we'll need to take to conquer my fear of intimacy," she corrected, leaving the table and moving to stand beside him at the counter.

"I knew it," he said smugly, and she didn't deny it. She *was* thinking about sex, hot, steamy, delicious sex with Tristan, and orgasms, plenty of orgasms, once she learned how to let herself go.

"If you don't stop looking like that, we're going to move to the next item on your list, and we'll probably stay there for a while."

"Works for me," she declared, not minding one bit if they decided to forgo tackling her fear of knives right now, or ever.

"But if we do work on this one now, that'll take one thing off your list, and give us more time to accomplish the next one."

"Okay." As if she'd argue with that.

He grabbed a knife from the block and held it in his hand. "You'll tell me if you start to feel anything out of the ordinary, right?"

Chantelle nodded. In spite of their sexual banter, she hadn't lost sight of what they were about to do. And she also wasn't fooled by Tristan's talk about sex and orgasms. They'd have to conquer that fear soon, but he was using the tantalizing subject to keep her mind off the sharp knife in his hand.

"I can do it," she said. "I have to."

Tristan put the knife in his left hand, then placed his right hand over hers. "Let me help you."

She nodded, accepting his offer, and he eased the knife into her hand, then closed her fingers around the handle. The wood wasn't cool or warm or anything; it was simply *there* in her hand, and it anchored the long sharp blade protruding from her grasp—the same way Romero's blade had looked back then in his grasp. Her throat tightened, chest clenched.

"You okay?" he asked, positioning the boudin on the board and slowly guiding her hand, and the knife, toward the center of the two links.

Chantelle tried to focus on the present, on the tenderness of his hand over hers, the incredible heat and strength of his body pressing against hers, the spicy scent of the sausage. She could nearly taste the Cajun specialty on her tongue. She concentrated on all of this—so she wouldn't concentrate so much on the knife in her hand.

But her pulse quickened. Her breathing grew erratic. And a thick haze cloaked the room.

"Chantelle, are you okay?" Tristan leaned against her, his mouth very close to her ear as he spoke, and she nodded. How was she going to conquer this fear if she didn't deal with it? She tried to think about everything *except* the knife. If she was going to get rid of this ghost—a ghost that wanted her dead—then she had to face this fear head on.

"I'm okay," she lied.

He helped her make the first cut, then he lined up the links of sausage on the board. "You're sure?"

She nodded again, still lying. "You want them sliced in half, right?"

"Yeah, but I'll cut them in half. You're doing great, but I can tell that you're not comfortable." He paused, then added, "This may have been too much too soon."

"No," Chantelle said, not wanting to stop now. She needed to strike this one off the list, and she needed to get it done tonight. The longer she waited, the more opportunity her ghost would have to accomplish *his* goal. "I want to. Here, let me do it on my own." She turned her head to look at him. "I'm fine. I can do it."

He hesitated. "Okay," he finally said, but she knew Tristan suspected the truth, that merely touching the knife almost made her sick, made the past seem all too real, all too near again.

She hoped he didn't notice that her arm literally

trembled as she moved it away from his. "I can do it," she said again. "Now scoot away a bit. Too many cooks in the kitchen spoil the soup, you know."

He smiled and then leaned against the counter a few feet away. "You don't have to conquer them all tonight, you know."

"I know, but if I do conquer this one, then, like you said, we'll have more time for the next one. Intimacy, wasn't it?" Her voice *appeared* calm. Good.

"Not going to argue with you there," he teased, watching as she placed the knife into the center of the first link and cut down its length.

Chantelle forced the knife to remain steady and tried to keep her attention on what she was doing, but it was exceedingly difficult. She no longer had Tristan's steady hand guiding the way, no longer had the warmth of him behind her, around her, enveloping her and giving her strength. And now she realized she desperately needed that strength. Without it, she felt *alone*. And as she lifted the knife after that first cut, she noticed the way the blade caught the light and remembered…

The knife was cold against her throat. Her eyes were covered with the blindfold, but that knife was there—it was always there—and as real as the one currently in her hand. He held it against her and if she tried to get away, or if she even made an effort to move back from the cold steel of the deadly blade, he'd push the tip against her throat, piercing her skin, making her scream…

Like back then, Chantelle felt the hatred, the vicious hatred of the man yielding the knife, the disgusting man who did such horrible things…

She started to shake and immediately sensed another presence against her back, but it wasn't Tristan. It was way too cold to be Tristan.

Her wrist. Something circled her wrist, something chilling and scary and...

It lifted her hand, and she tried to drop the knife from her grasp, tried to uncurl her fingers from the handle, but she couldn't. That same icy strength held her palm against the handle, and then pushed the blade upward, in an arc with an obvious final goal.

"Chantelle." Tristan started toward her.

A second knife in the block moved out of its slot and hurled through the air toward Tristan.

"Chantelle!" he yelled, jerking to the side. The blade barely missed his right shoulder.

"Tristan!" She fought to control her arm, but lost her tug-of-war against something she couldn't see, against a spirit who wouldn't yield. The presence brought the blade to her throat and held it there, against the side of her neck, so close that she could feel her pulse thumping madly against the blade. "Tristan, stop him!"

Tristan lunged forward, grabbing her wrist and yanking it from her throat. Her arm was wrenched away sharply, sending a piercing stab of pain from her shoulder to her fingertips, but the action caused her grip to relax and the knife dropped loudly into the sink.

The cold left at once, and Chantelle collapsed against Tristan. "He knows. That ghost *knows* what the Romeros did to us back then. He knows, and he's trying to do it again."

Tristan's heart thundered against her ear as he held

her to his chest, or was she simply hearing her own heart beating?

"He's gone, right?"

She nodded. "He left as soon as you got the knife out of my hand. I can feel him when he comes, and I can tell the second he leaves."

"God, Chantelle, did I hurt you?" Tristan asked, moving his hand to her shoulder and gently pressing it with his fingers.

"Not nearly as much as he'd have hurt me if you hadn't gotten that knife away. If you hadn't been here, do you think he would've actually used that knife? Or made me use it on myself? That's what he was going to do, wasn't it?"

Tristan's rage bristled from within him as he spoke. "No, that's definitely not what he was doing, not this time. If he'd wanted to use that knife on you or make you use it on yourself, he could have—I didn't get to you fast enough to stop that, dammit. But he didn't, and I think I know why. Like Jake said, he's feeding off your fear. He didn't want to hurt you, not yet, but he wanted to scare the shit out of you. And the only way we can stop him from accomplishing that, and then doing worse, is to find a way to help you deal with your fears—quickly."

"I'm not ready for knives," she said, and refused to even look in the direction of the one she knew was in the sink, or the other one on the floor that the ghost had flung at Tristan, or even the ones still perched in the knife block on the counter. She didn't even want to be in the same *room* with any of them.

Tristan seemed to understand what she was thinking. "Come on. Let's get out of here, go upstairs."

"What are we going to do?"

"We're going to regroup and concentrate on an area that we nearly succeeded in before."

She knew he was talking about the two of them being together, but she'd been through way too much in the past twenty-four hours to even consider being intimate with anyone now. Even Tristan.

"I…can't."

10

"I'M NOT ABOUT to ask you to have sex now," Tristan said, stroking a hand down her hair as he spoke. "I know you need to master your fears, but I also know there's only so much one person can take in a day, and I'd say you've had more than your share of emotional turmoil for this one. However, I still think we can work toward conquering your fear of intimacy."

"How?" she asked, her head still resting against his chest. Have mercy, she was so tired, so drained. Fighting for her life—with an enraged ghost, no less—had that effect on her. Go figure.

"We won't have sex," he reiterated, his hand now beneath her hair and caressing her back. "But we can still help you learn how to let your body get lost in the emotions of intimacy, without remembering the emotions from abuse."

"How?" she asked again.

"Come on," he said, taking her hand and leading her out of the kitchen.

"Where are we going?"

"We need to do a little exploration."

She couldn't fight the grin that tugged at her lips as she followed him up to the second floor and into a bedroom at the end of the hall, merely three doors down from Adeline Vicknair's infamous sitting room. He noted the suitcases on the floor and her computer bag on an ancient desk. "Gage and Kayla got everything, I see." Then he turned toward her and asked, "Do you trust me?"

"Yes." There was no doubt about that. If she didn't trust him, she wouldn't be here alone in this house with him, and she wouldn't have asked him to sleep with her after Dax's wedding. At that time, she'd believed he might be the only man who could help her lose herself in the beauty of sex. Truthfully she still did. She hadn't been able to let go of the past then, but the fact that she quivered now, merely from looking at him and knowing he was fiercely determined to give her everything she needed, physically and emotionally, made her believe even more that if any guy could make her lose control, Tristan was the one.

She stood near the doorway, and Tristan reached past her, closed the door and turned the lock.

"So you won't have to worry about privacy," he said. Then he took her hand and silently led her across the room.

Chantelle was surprised when they moved past the bed and toward another door. He opened it and they entered a bathroom. The fixtures were brass and crystal, definitely antique, and tiny white square tiles covered the floor. One of the faucets leaked, and the sound of the water dripping from the spout echoed off the walls, but instead of sounding eerie, it sounded homey. Chantelle felt good in here, relaxed.

A beige curtain hung from a brass ceiling rod, and Tristan pushed it aside to reveal a vintage clawfoot tub.

He turned the faucets and started the water running, then held a hand beneath the stream to test the heat. When he was satisfied with the temperature, he turned to Chantelle.

She looked at him. "That tub is a little small for both of us, don't you think?" she asked.

He tugged his T-shirt from his jeans and pulled it up and over his head. Chantelle was treated to an awe-inspiring display of abs and pecs and...Tristan. His skin was more darkly tanned than she remembered, presumably from working on the plantation without his shirt— that image made her breath catch.

"I was hoping you'd ask me to join you," he said. "Glad to see we're thinking alike."

"What *are* you thinking, Tristan?" She looked at those green eyes, more emerald now, the way they'd been on that night they'd made love; it was the color they turned when he was aroused. She let her gaze ease downward, to the top of his jeans, resting low on his hips. Was he aroused now? She slid her gaze to the front of those jeans and knew for certain. A prominent bulge pressed against the denim, reminding Chantelle of just how impressive he was without his clothes, without *all* of his clothes. "You said we weren't going to have sex tonight, so what are we doing? Just so I know."

The water in the tub neared the top, and he reached over and shut off the taps. "I thought you could use a nice hot bath to help you relax."

"And you'll be with me, while I'm relaxing."

"I'll be with you always, until that ghost is gone. Whether you're bathing or sleeping or anything else, I'm not leaving you."

She thought to ask how she'd conquer the fear of being alone if he never left her, but that wasn't what was most important right now. Right now she wanted to know how he expected the two of them to take a bath together in that tiny tub and not have sex, particularly when he was obviously thinking about and wanting sex.

"Chantelle," he said, "you're staring."

She swallowed. Yes, she was staring at his jeans, or more precisely, at what was barely contained within them. "Won't this be difficult for you?"

"Having you naked against me, you bathing me and me bathing you, without having sex? Hell, yeah, it'll be difficult."

You bathing me and me bathing you. She hadn't really thought about that. But she did like the sound of it.

"But it'll be worth it, in spite of how difficult it is, because we'll be doing it right this time," he continued.

"We did something wrong last time?"

"No, we didn't—*I* did. I treated you the same way I'd treat any other—" He stopped and shook his head. "No, that's not true. I did treat you differently than other women, because you *are* different to me, Chantelle. You've always been different, from the first time we met last year and fought with each other about your doggedness."

"*My* doggedness?"

He smirked, stepped closer to her, and ran his fingers against her cheek. "Okay, *our* doggedness," he said. "But what I'm trying to say is that I should have thought more about you, about all you'd been through, that night when we were together. I mean, I did think about it—to a point. I knew you wanted me to sleep with you to help you push away the pain of the past, but what I didn't realize was that you needed more than sex with the traditional amount of foreplay."

She cocked her head. "There's a traditional amount of foreplay?"

He scrubbed his hand down his face. "That didn't come out right."

"I hope not," Chantelle said, but she smiled. He really was trying to get something important across, even if he wasn't doing a great a job of it. "Wanna try again?"

"I'd better. What I want to say is that in order to combat the memories of your past, you need to really experience how two people *learn* each other, how you and I can learn each other, enjoying each other's bodies and building up to the kind of lovemaking where we know each other so completely, so acutely, that every time I touch you, not only do you feel it, but I feel it, too, because it touches my soul. And every time you touch me, not only will I feel it—"

"But I'll feel it, too, because it touches my soul," she whispered.

He nodded. "That's what I believe you need before we have sex again. You need to be a part of me and I need to be a part of you, so that when you do get lost in the moment, and you start to let yourself soar, nothing holds you back."

"That doesn't sound very temporary," she said.

His mouth tensed slightly, but she noticed. "Temporary?"

"We're trying to get rid of this ghost, and I want to, but it sounds like you're talking about something more." More emotional. More long-term. More committed. More...permanent. She shivered, realizing he'd effectively reminded her of the one thing she feared that wasn't on her list. *Love.*

He smiled, but it seemed a bit forced. "Chantelle, I'm trying to help you learn to let yourself go, but the only way I see that happening is for you to let me get closer to you, and for you to get closer to me."

"You said for me to become a part of you, and you a part of me," she reminded him.

"Because I believe that's how close we need to be for you to overcome your fear." He inhaled, then let the breath out slowly, frustration replacing the desire she'd seen in his eyes only moments ago. "Chantelle, he wants you dead, and if we don't figure out how to deal with this, how to help you work through your fears, then he's going to get stronger. I barely got that knife away this time, and I'm thinking if we don't weaken him before he tries again, I might not be able to stop him. And I couldn't handle it if something happened to you." Tristan put his hands on her shoulders and stepped so close she could literally sense his resolve to stop the ghost before he hurt her again. "If you aren't comfortable with this," he said, indicating the tub filled with steaming water, "then we won't even try it. I'll admit, I was trying to think of some way to connect intimately without climbing in bed and without trying to have sex when you clearly weren't ready. This seemed like a good idea." He shrugged. "Hell, I'm a guy. Any idea that involves being naked with a beautiful woman seems like a damn good one."

She laughed at that, then rose on her toes and pressed her mouth to his. He accepted what she offered, but didn't push for more, his mouth moving against hers and eliciting a strong yearning within her. She slid her arms around him and moved her hands across the corded muscles of his back. Without really thinking about what she was doing, she let the heat, the sensation flowing through her, take control, and she curved her body into his, her center rubbing against the hard bulge in his jeans. Then she deepened the kiss, perusing his mouth with her tongue and relishing the taste of him, the strength of him. She moaned softly, and he slid his hands to her bottom and pressed her more firmly against his hard length.

When they broke the kiss, she admitted, "You're right. It's going to take more than mere sex for me to let myself go, and that's what was missing that night we were together. As much as I cared about you as a person, and as much as I wanted you as a man, you weren't truly a part of me, so it was just sex. This time, for me to let go and to get rid of my ghost, I have to need you, only you. To get my mind off the past, it has to be about *us,* the two of us and only us."

"That's what I'm thinking," Tristan said, his voice deep and raspy and extremely sexy.

"And we're going to start getting to know each other that way by taking a bath?"

His mouth crooked up at one side. "Like I said, any idea that has both of us naked seems like a damn good one to me."

"Then by all means, let's put the idea to the test."

11

TRISTAN HAD NEVER DONE anything this difficult in his life, and he wasn't talking about undressing Chantelle and then bathing her without having sex, though that was one for the record books. Oh no, he was talking about keeping his mind on the two of them when what he really wanted to do was find that damn ghost and tear him apart. Not that that was even possible. The guy was already dead.

Chantelle leaned her head against his chest, her blond hair in long wet ringlets, some pressed to his skin and some floating in the water. She was so beautiful, so sexy, so enchanting. Her feet rested against either side of the faucet, the pale-pink polish on her toes capturing his attention. Tiny water droplets trickled down her feet, then continued down the portion of her leg that wasn't submerged. He wanted her desperately—but not enough to risk making her remember the past and giving that damn ghost more power. No, his idea had been pretty much on the mark—get her mind on intimacy, but not on the actual act of sex. He needed her to learn his body, and her own, and fully enjoy both before they tried to have sex again. But damn if it wasn't the death of him, having her naked, her cute little bottom pressing against his erection as they soaked in the cramped tub.

And how could he totally enjoy this when his mind kept remembering that knife at her throat and the helplessness of knowing that all that ghost had to do was press it into her flesh…

"Tristan," she whispered, and he looked down to see her eyes closed, her mouth parted. His dick pushed against her, and she smiled softly. "I feel that."

"I'd think something was seriously wrong if you didn't."

She grinned, opened her eyes and tilted her head to look at him. "You know, we haven't even started bathing yet."

Tristan didn't need a reminder. He was currently running his palms up and down the length of her arms, massaging in slow lazy circles, but he wanted to touch her like this everywhere.

He'd told the truth; he wanted to learn her body and let her learn his, to explore her sensitive erogenous zones and discover what she liked most, let her learn what he liked most, and what they liked together. He would help her get there, to have an orgasm that rocked her to her toes—and pushed that ghost one step further away from hurting her. And he'd start right now. "Hand me the soap."

Reaching for the soap dish, she scooted forward, which caused her behind to rub his cock. Then she turned, which wasn't easy, given that they filled the tub completely, and Tristan was rewarded with one of the most exquisite images he'd ever seen. Chantelle, her long blond spirals tumbling past her shoulders and parted by her full breasts, rose-tinted tips wet and shimmering. He wanted to lick them dry, suck them until she screamed his name, feel her abdomen flex in direct response to his mouth on her breast and know that he could take her where she needed to go.

"Me first," she said, taking a washcloth from beside the tub and dipping it in the water. Then she lathered the soap in the cloth and looked up at him, sky-blue eyes studying him intently as she leaned toward him. "Close your eyes."

Tristan did as she said, sliding his eyes closed, which naturally intensified the awareness of his other senses. He felt her skin rub against his as she rested one hand against his chest and used the other to wash his face. The sudsy cloth slid across his hairline, then eased over his forehead and down the bridge of his nose.

"Keep them closed," she whispered, gently easing the cloth across his eyes before continuing to form small circles on each cheek, and then his jaw and his lips, the tiny bubbles tingling on his skin. She rinsed them away with the same care, massaging his face with the cloth as she did so. "Open them."

Tristan blinked to free the water from his lashes, then saw Chantelle, lathering the cloth again. She was smiling softly and appeared content, as if this was totally natural for her, bathing him in the tiny clawfoot tub. He held up one arm and then the other as she washed them, then twisted around as much as the cramped space allowed while she attempted to bathe him. She washed his back, her breasts rubbing against him with the action, and his cock hardened to the point of pain. Eventually, she'd bathed everything except the part of him that ached for her touch. At last her attention moved to his penis, rock hard and prominently on display in the water.

Chantelle lathered the washcloth again, then stroked his erection with the sudsy fabric. She slid it down the shaft, which was getting harder and longer as she worked, and then rubbed it over his testicles. "Tristan," she whispered, her gaze focused on his cock.

"Yeah?"

"Are you…will this make you come?"

He smiled at the question, but was also thrilled that she definitely had no ghosts on her mind now. "Maybe when I was a teen it'd have done the trick, but now…no."

"You need me for that. You'd need to be inside me?"

Tristan hadn't realized just how very little she understood about the whole scenario of sex, but how would she know more? When most kids were going through the process of learning about sex and were intrigued by it, she'd been sexually abused. Therefore, as an older teenager and an adult, she'd seen sex as an unwanted assault, and something that wouldn't—couldn't—be pleasurable. That night, when she and Tristan had been together, she'd nearly seen the beauty of it, but the horror of her past had taken that near-perfect night and ruined it.

Tristan hated the Romeros for doing this to her, for leaving her so vulnerable, so scared, so unable to experience pleasure the way every woman should.

"Isn't that right?" she asked, easing away from him and dipping the cloth back in the water. She kept her eyes on the wet fabric, and then the soap, as she rubbed it against the washcloth.

Tristan reached for the cloth and slid it from her hands, and finally those blue eyes looked up at him.

"You'd need to be inside me?" she asked again.

"It's my turn, right?" Tristan indicated the soapy washcloth.

She nodded. "But I still want to know the answer to my question."

"I'll tell you everything you want to know, but I'm also going to do my part bathing you before the water gets cold." And he wanted more time to formulate his answer. How much did she know? How much did she need to learn? And how could he tell her without making her feel uncomfortable for being a twenty-three-year-old woman who knew virtually no more than a kid about sex.

She smiled, leaned toward him and closed her eyes. "Does a man have to be inside a woman to come?" she repeated. "I know a boy can get there by thinking about it, or by…"

The basics. She wanted to know the basics of what made a guy come, and what didn't. Okay, this wouldn't be the most comfortable of conversations, but it wasn't something he couldn't handle. "Masturbating," Tristan supplied, since she seemed to be having difficulty with the word, or perhaps with the thought of him doing it.

She nodded again while Tristan gently washed her face, then rinsed the soap away.

"Yes," he said. "Boys come quite easily, in fact, by merely thinking about it, or dreaming about it, or by masturbating." He grinned. "Hell, a teenage boy can nearly get there from looking at a girl fully clothed, just from watching the way she moves."

Chantelle pried one eye open. "Speaking from experience?"

"I haven't been a teenager for ten years now, so I have a hard time recalling." He moved the cloth over her throat and then to her breasts. They were undeniably large for her small frame, and he enjoyed the heaviness of them within his palms, and the way the tips grew even firmer and turned a darker rose as he washed them.

"I think you do recall it," she said, probably completely unaware of how sexy her smile was at this moment and how sexy her body was at this moment—at *all* moments. "Tristan?"

"Yeah."

"Are you nearly there now?"

"You tell me." He nodded toward his penis, jutting toward her and merely a short distance away from those golden curls between her thighs.

"Is this hard for you?" she asked, concerned. "Bathing me?"

"This—" he again indicated his erection "—is hard for you." He grinned and she laughed.

"Want me to finish?" She reached for the cloth. "I didn't think about how difficult this would be for you, and I can bathe myself." The corners of her mouth dipped down, and she added, barely above a whisper, "I do want to be with you again, Tristan, the way we were that night, but I don't want to disappoint you again."

"For the record, you didn't disappoint me then. I was irritated with myself for not realizing until the next morning that you were faking it, and then I was even more irritated because I hadn't been able to get you there."

"It wasn't your fault."

"No, it wasn't, at least not in the sense that I was doing anything wrong, but it was my fault for not realizing that we were moving way too fast for you. I won't let that happen again, which means we're going to take our time now and let you build your trust in our intimacy and learn gradually how much your body can enjoy everything involved with sex. The next time we're together, you're going to feel it everywhere, I promise." Tristan had no idea if she understood the magnitude of his promise, but *he* did; the next time he was with Chantelle Bedeau, she *would* feel it everywhere—in her heart, her body and her soul. "So, while I wouldn't mind watching you bathe yourself, I'd much rather do the job on my own. And it isn't going to kill me to think about how good it will be the next time we're together as I do it."

He moved the cloth down her abdomen, and Chantelle leaned back in the tub, sliding her center farther away from him, which was probably good, because they were entirely too close for comfort, or for Tristan's comfort, anyway. He did want to be inside her, but only when she was ready for him, and only when they were close enough that she wouldn't see what they were sharing as merely sex. When he was with Chantelle again, he'd be making love. The realization both intrigued him and scared the hell out of him.

Keeping a tight rein on his increasing desire, Tristan continued bathing her, but he didn't miss the opportunity to take note of each quickening of her breath, each tensing of her muscles, each indication of an erogenous zone that he would explore more thoroughly when they made love. Chantelle had many sensitive areas, and as he'd learned the night of Dax's wedding, she was extremely receptive to his touch. Her nipples budded almost instantly with the softest brush of his fingers. The tender spot behind each ear elicited a quickening pulse and a gasp of impending pleasure. He also noticed that when he rubbed the sudsy cloth just beneath her navel, her legs parted slightly and her hips arched upward in the water. He'd investigate that erogenous area more thoroughly soon—with his mouth. That particular spot would invite a path of sweet kisses to her clitoris, and if Tristan had brought her where she needed to go and had taken the time to bring her along emotionally, moving her beyond the pain of her past, maybe, just maybe, he'd bring her to a delicious climax with his tongue.

"Tristan," she said, eyeing his cock, which had gotten harder and longer, the head visible now above the water.

"I can't stop what I'm thinking," he admitted. "But I can wait until you're ready."

"Maybe we could try tonight," she said, and her eyes never left his penis.

"No." He tilted her face to look directly at him. "We're not going at my pace, Chantelle, because like most men, I'm pretty much always ready, willing and able to rise to the occasion." He was trying to lighten the tension he could see in her eyes. She wanted to please him, wanted to give him what he wanted, but she was still scared, and he didn't want to scare Chantelle in any way. There was another male, albeit a dead one, doing enough of that.

"I could still help you come, even if we didn't—"

"Not tonight, *chère*," he drawled, though his dick begged to differ. "Besides, the water is growing cold and we've both bathed now." He pushed against the sides of the tub to stand, grabbed a towel and dried off, then wrapped it around his waist and reached for her.

"Come on, let's get some sleep. Tomorrow we'll try to go a little further toward this."

"Toward having sex, you mean," she said, letting him towel her off as she spoke. Then she took the towel and tucked it around her, and ran her fingers through her hair to loosen the tangles. "Truthfully, Tristan, I don't think we can wait. I mean, we can't go just 'a little further' each day, because we don't know when he's going to come back."

"He gets stronger because of your fears, so if we work toward overcoming them, or at least one of them, then that should keep him at bay." Tristan hoped that the statement held merit. He'd never dealt with a renegade ghost before and he honestly had no idea how long they had to get rid of him. But conquering Chantelle's fear was the only means they possessed for eliminating him, and he knew that it'd take more than a day to defeat the fears that had ruled much of her life.

Tristan was a bit dismayed that they'd inadvertently ended up back on the subject of her ghost. Did thinking about him, talking about him, give him strength, too? Would that enable him to try to get to her tonight while she slept? And what would Tristan do if he did? He couldn't hurt the damn spirit. Until Chantelle overpowered her fears, Tristan had no means whatsoever of stopping him.

Chantelle used another towel to squeeze the excess water from her hair, then she ran her fingers through the curls again. "I don't think I have all the time in the world to do this, though," she said. "I know your grandmother didn't give us a deadline for when we have to send him on his way or anything like that, but I can't help but think that the longer he's here, the stronger he'll become. It just seems like I need to face my fears, all of them, before he takes advantage of my weakness and I end up not being around to tell anyone about it."

Her bluntness reminded him of the Chantelle he'd met last year, the one determined to make her sister's killer pay, and the one who would argue with him until she got her way. This was the person she'd wanted to be, he now realized, but it wasn't the person she was. She wanted to be fearless, independent, capable of anything, but the Romeros had squelched that fiery spirit and it now only occasionally found its way to the surface. Had their interaction tonight, bathing and talking and getting closer, helped her boldness come out? If it had, Tristan was exceedingly thankful. Because at this moment, she did seem as though she was ready to move forward, to battle her fears—and to become closer to Tristan in the process.

He was more than ready.

She picked up the hair dryer from the counter, then placed it back down and shook her head. "I'm going to let it dry while I sleep." She paused, then added, "Tristan, that ghost isn't the only reason I don't want to waste time. I want you. I'll let you know what I can handle or what I can't. So if I want to be with you that way, then I expect you to let me."

God, he loved the determination, the resoluteness, that was pure Chantelle. "We'll go as far as you want."

She smiled her approval. "Good."

12

"I DON'T WANT to wait." She took his hand and led him out of the bathroom and toward the bed. "Please, Tristan." She untucked the towel from her chest and let it fall to the floor. His towel was still wrapped around his waist, and his erection pushed prominently against the material. He obviously wanted her as much as she wanted him, but would he let them have what they both wanted? "I'm not afraid of this," she said, just in case he needed her to say it.

"Chantelle, if we try to do too much too fast, and it reminds you of—"

"I know. If the past starts creeping in, then I'm only going to make him stronger, but how will we know whether I can overcome that if we don't try?"

"I do think we should try. I'm dying for us to try," he said, smiling. "But remember what happened in the Jeep when we kissed. My mind was on the here and now, but I wasn't able to keep yours there completely, and when you thought about what happened before, he tossed that rock at the windshield and ended up hurting you. Chantelle, I want you more than I've ever wanted anything or anyone, but I'm not willing to give him ammunition to hurt you again."

"He can only hurt me if I let my fear take control." She moved her hand to his chest, let her fingers pass over the hard ridges of his abdomen. His muscles twitched beneath her touch, and the erection, barely contained by the towel, moved. Chantelle couldn't stop if she tried. She had to have him. Her fingers trembled as she eased them to the edge of the towel, then pulled it free.

She moved onto the bed and her entire body shuddered as he followed her. But the shuddering wasn't due to fear; it was due to need. She needed this, needed him.

"I'm not thinking of anything else now, Tristan. Only you and how much I want you."

His erection nudged her thigh, and she had no doubt he didn't want to wait, not really, but she could see the apprehension in his eyes. He wasn't sure she was ready. Her fears were once again threatening to keep them from doing what they both so desperately wanted to do. How could she convince him to stop waiting and give her the orgasm her body burned for?

She blinked, thinking that perhaps she knew what would convince him that they didn't need to wait any longer. "That night, after Dax's wedding, there was something that nearly got me there, and I didn't have any thoughts of the past when you touched me that way."

His throat pulsed as he swallowed. "I'm listening."

She took his hand, guiding it down her abdomen and then between her thighs. "When you kissed me there, licked me there, that was as close as I've ever been. And there aren't any thoughts of the past involved, because you're the only one who's ever touched me that way."

His green eyes grew darker, and his fingers touched her wet folds. She opened her legs, sliding one between his thighs and feeling his erection hard against her leg. She rubbed against it and closed her eyes to imagine that long hard length deep within her. If Tristan saw that she could climax with him, from his hand and his mouth, then maybe he'd see that she was ready for more, for everything.

"Kiss me there," she said, lifting her hips to push her center against his hand. "Help me, Tristan. Make me come. Help me feel what I've never felt before."

He pushed the sheets to the floor, then moved her to the middle of the bed, her head resting on a pillow and her body completely nude.

"Please," she said. "Don't make me wait, Tristan. I want to feel it." She watched him move down the mattress, his face near her thigh.

"You're sure, Chantelle," he whispered as he nipped at her thigh.

"Yes."

He planted one soft kiss against her clitoris, and Chantelle gasped in sheer pleasure, then he paused, looked up at her with those intense green eyes and said, "On one condition."

No. There was no way he could stop now, not when she needed this so much. "What condition?"

"That you don't close your eyes. I want you to watch, Chantelle. Watch me taste you, watch me enjoy you, and…"

"And remember that this is here and now, you and me, and that what's happening right now is all that matters," she said, the words rapidly delivered because of her growing need for what she knew he could give her.

"Yes."

"I promise," she said, then to her absolute delight, Tristan's palms pressed against her thighs, easing them outward to completely open her intimate center for him. He kissed her clitoris again, and her hips lifted involuntarily, and she burned with need.

His tongue slid down her folds, while the tension within her increased, her hips moving fluidly as she pressed against that incredible mouth, giving him everything he wanted, and giving herself the same—everything *she* wanted. He took his time, humming his contentment as he kissed, nibbled and licked his way back to her clitoris, and by the time he drew the aching nub into his mouth, Chantelle knew there wouldn't be anything holding her back this time. She was so close, so ready, so eager to feel what was nearly within reach.

He stroked the tingling sensitive spot with his tongue, massaging it in the most intimate way. Chantelle let the blissful sensation, the immeasurable pleasure, hold her at the brink, teetering on the edge of release—longing to have what was so incredibly close.

Her breath caught, and her heels pressed into the mattress as his fingers delved into her core and his mouth sucked hard on her clit. The tension spiraled from her very being, building to a painful need, yearning for release, aching for…

His teeth grazed her tender nub, and Chantelle plummeted over the edge, shudders of pleasure claiming her entire being as her world changed completely, immersed with the present, with what was happening here and now, with this moment, this climax…this incredible man.

13

NORMALLY TRISTAN WAS a light sleeper, and the rapping on the bedroom door would have easily roused him. But after Chantelle had finally learned to let go and experience the climax she deserved, she hadn't wanted to stop at one. Neither had Tristan. Therefore, he'd been up the majority of the night helping the beautiful woman beside him have more orgasms than he could count—and all of them with his mouth. He could only imagine the force of her first climax with him deep inside her tight center. Tristan believed she was ready for that. Obviously there had been no thoughts of the past last night, and he thought her fear of intimacy had been conquered. There was no reason they couldn't have everything. He'd pulled her closer, falling into such a deep contented sleep that even the persistent pounding didn't disturb him. Chantelle, however, wasn't as immune to the invasion.

"Hey, sleepy," she whispered, kissing him awake. "I think someone wants us to get up."

He smiled at her, and instantly recalled the way her body had clenched, her eyes glazed, and she'd screamed his name—his name—when she came. He couldn't wait until she experienced all of that and more…with him deep, deep inside her.

"I'd ask what you're thinking, but I'm sure I know," she said, and he noticed that her lower lip was a bit swollen, undoubtedly from biting it when she climaxed. He inched toward her, ran his tongue along her lip, then slid it into her mouth for a thorough kiss.

Chantelle smiled against his mouth, then laughed when the knocking continued, but much, much louder, and then Nanette's voice joined the sound.

"Tristan, I've *tried* to be patient, but it's two in the afternoon, and I need some questions answered," she said, still banging her fist on the door as she spoke.

He climbed out of bed, and Chantelle's attention immediately moved to his penis pushing against his boxers.

"Next time, you're coming, too," she said softly, as though Nanette might hear her over the sound of her pounding. "I'm ready for more, for you inside me, Tristan."

He really liked the sound of that. He kissed her, then slipped on his jeans in an attempt to disguise his erection from Nan's perceptive gaze. He hadn't even *tried* to enter Chantelle throughout the night, because it simply hadn't been the right time. But he agreed with her now; she was ready, and so was he. As long as he could keep her attention focused on what they were doing, on the present, not the past, he believed she could enjoy every aspect of sex without remembering the abuse and causing that insidious ghost to return. After seeing the way she let go last night, he thought it was possible, no, probable, that she could really, truly make love with him.

He walked to the door, opened it, and was nearly hit with Nanette's busy fist, moving forward for another rapping session. "Come to bring me coffee in bed?" he asked, but he knew better. She wasn't holding a mug, and Nanette wasn't exactly the type to bring Tristan, or any other male, coffee in bed. He imagined that one day she'd have a husband who would bring it to her and dote on her every wish, assuming she ever found a guy who didn't piss her off. So far, that hadn't happened.

"Coffee in bed?" she snapped. "As if. For one thing, it's two in the afternoon, a little late for morning coffee. And for another, I'm not Grandma Adeline, and why she always brought you coffee in bed every time you spent the night here is beyond me."

"She brought it to me because she knew it made me feel special and I would start my day off in a good mood," he said. "She never brought you coffee, Nan?" He knew the answer, but hell, she was fun to tease.

"Phfft, Grandma Adeline was a sucker for all boys. Thank God, I didn't take after her there," Nanette said, crossing her arms over her chest.

"I'll say," Tristan muttered, and she cut her green eyes at him as she entered the room without regard to the fact that Chantelle was in his bed. She glanced at the gorgeous blonde and explained, "Sorry, but I couldn't wait anymore."

"No problem. We need to get up and have something to eat, anyway."

Tristan's stomach promptly growled, and Chantelle grinned. "See?" she said.

"I'm glad that the two of you slept in and that you seem to be in much better spirits this morning," Nan said to Chantelle. Better spirits. An interesting way of describing the way Chantelle looked. He supposed it was a fairly accurate description, since she'd wanted an orgasm for a very long time, and she'd had not one, but several toe-curling climaxes, courtesy of him.

He smiled and she smiled back. *Mon Dieu,* she was beautiful.

"But Gage called and said he and Kayla are on their way and that Kayla needs to talk specifically to Chantelle and that she didn't want to do it over the phone. He said it was urgent and that it involves her ghost."

"What about him?" Tristan asked, his attention shifting abruptly from the woman in his bed to the spirit determined to hurt her. Wasn't going to happen, no matter what he had to do to stop it.

"Gage wouldn't say anything specific, but it sounded important, so I thought I should make sure both of you were up when he gets here. Just so you know, I reread your book last night, Chantelle, to see if I could find anything that I thought would make a spirit angry," Nanette said.

"And?" Chantelle looked inquiringly at Tristan's older cousin.

"Couldn't find a thing. I don't get it."

"Neither do I," Chantelle said. "I can't imagine why Evan and Lorelei's story would upset a ghost so much."

"Well, maybe Kayla thought of something." Nan glanced at the clock by the bed. "Gage called a half hour ago from his apartment, so they should be here in around twenty minutes."

"We'll be ready," Tristan said.

"And something else," Nan added. "I want to know what happened last night."

"What do you mean?" Tristan asked. Even if Nanette

had heard Chantelle scream when she came, she wouldn't mention it, would she?

"In the kitchen. When Jenee and I got back from the firehouse, we found sausage links left out on the counter, a knife on the floor by the stove and another one in the sink. You're not the best at cleaning up after yourself," she said to Tristan, "but I have a feeling that this time it wasn't merely messy housekeeping, was it?"

Tristan would rather have explained what happened with Chantelle's ghost in private, when Chantelle wasn't listening a few feet away and undoubtedly re-membering how her ghost had attacked both of them in the kitchen. But there was no way he was going to leave her alone for any reason, so anything he said to Nanette would have to be said in front of her. He looked at her, saw those blue eyes focused on him with absolute trust, and believed she could handle whatever he said and whatever that ghost did. She was stronger than he'd thought, and he was glad of it. Perhaps they could conquer more of her fears today and then send that damn ghost to hell where he belonged.

He told Nanette about Grandma Adeline's message and about everything that had happened in the kitchen with Chantelle's ghost.

Nanette was clearly shocked by what had happened, but true to her take-charge mentality, she wasted no time defining what she could do to help. "I told Tristan's men at the firehouse that I'd bring them a big pot of gumbo tonight for dinner since they made enough progress on the house for us to be ready for Roussel and his committee's inspection tomorrow. I'll have to chop onions, sausage and peppers for it, and I'll get you to help me, Chantelle. We'll take it slow, and Tristan can help you until you're comfortable with slicing on your own, but we'll work on that fear today. We'll get you past it—there's no way we can let that ghost hurt you. He's not going to win. I won't let him."

Tristan grinned. Nanette was at her best when she was in bitch mode, and right now, her nostrils flared, green eyes blazed and she looked ready to take on the world—or at least a rampant spirit. Worked for Tristan, and for Chantelle, from the way she smiled at Tristan's cousin.

"Sounds great," Chantelle said.

Tristan nodded his approval, and silently prayed that she was as ready as she believed. "We'll be down soon, before Kayla and Gage get here."

"I'll fix some sandwiches for lunch. I'm sure you're both starved," Nanette said, then turned and left.

As soon as Tristan closed the bedroom door, Jake appeared by the window. The ghost glowed even brighter than before, signifying he was getting closer to the time of his crossing.

"Jake, is everything okay?" Tristan asked.

Chantelle had been looking at Tristan, but now her attention followed his to the window where the ghost stood. "Jake is here?" she asked, and Tristan nodded.

"I need to know…" Jake started, then scrubbed his glowing hand down his face as though almost afraid to finish the sentence.

"What do you need to know?" Tristan asked.

"Right now, she knows I'm there. When the nurses are out of the room, she talks to me. And when I touch her, she knows. She moves her hand to the place I've touched and says my name."

Tristan nodded, knowing that loved ones typically sensed their beloved spirits.

"But after I cross, is that over? Will she still…will she ever feel me again?" Jake's jaw clenched as he braced for Tristan's reply.

"I'm going to let Chantelle answer that," Tristan said. "Her sister crossed over last year, and she would be able to explain it best."

"Explain?" Chantelle was unable to hear Jake's side of the conversation.

"Whether a living person still feels their loved one once they've crossed over."

Chantelle nodded, obviously understanding Jake's concerns. "Yes, I still feel Lillian watching over me, though it's not the same as when she was in the middle. It isn't as tangible anymore, but it's more like a comforting sensation, an awareness that I'm not alone, and that she's watching over me—and loves me."

Jake's mouth trembled as he smiled. "Thank you. I'm going back to her now. We only have one more day. And then…I'll watch over her and continue loving her always. I don't guess I'll see you again on this side," he said to Tristan. "So I suppose this is goodbye. Thank you again for…everything. And thank her for me, too." He nodded toward Chantelle, then turned and disappeared.

"He went back to her," Tristan said. "And he thanked you for answering his question."

"Was he okay with my answer?"

"Yes. That's what he needed to know. I'm sure you

helped him more than you can even imagine. I wish you could have seen his face—he was resolved to moving on, as long as he could still show Caroline his love."

"I'm glad." Her stomach growled loudly, and she climbed naked from the bed. "Amazing how multiple orgasms can work up your appetite."

Tristan grinned, happy to see her so content. Still...what if her ghost returned?

She started getting dressed, then caught his gaze and paused. "You're worried about me trying the knives again."

"I'd be lying if I said I'm not."

"I'll never know whether I can conquer that fear unless I try. And if I'm not ready, I'll stop."

"I just don't want you trying to accomplish too much too soon and giving him the upper hand."

"I don't plan to," she said, pulling her T-shirt over her head, then pulling those long blond curls through to tumble down her back. "If I start thinking about the past or if I sense him at all, I'll quit and tackle my fear of knives tomorrow."

Tristan knew that if she started thinking about the past or, God forbid, started sensing that ghost, then it'd be too late, because once that ghost got access to her, once his power was strong enough to hurt her, he wouldn't waste time.

And what if he wasn't content to just scare her next time?

14

CHANTELLE AND TRISTAN entered the kitchen to find two tall glasses of iced tea beside plates filled with thick, shrimp po'boy sandwiches, Zapp's potato chips and pickle spears. There was enough food on those two plates for at least four people.

"Paul Boudreaux brought your Jeep back this morning while you were sleeping," Nanette said as she washed dished. "I called and let Gerry know he could come pick up his truck, but he said he didn't need it right now and he'd get it sometime next week. Chantelle, Boudreaux said your car will take a while longer." She tilted her head toward the towering plates of food.

Chantelle's eyes widened at Tristan, but he wasn't looking at her; he was focused on his cousin.

"Okay, Nan, what's up?" His voice had converted to that commanding tone Chantelle heard every time she said something he didn't agree with.

Nanette exhaled audibly, then turned. "What do you mean?"

Chantelle had to give her an A for effort. The woman honestly looked as though she didn't know what he was talking about. But Tristan wasn't fooled.

"You cook when you're worried, which makes me

think you know more about Gage and Kayla's visit than you're letting on."

"I made sandwiches. That can hardly be classified as 'cooking.'"

Tristan sat down behind one of the plates and motioned to Chantelle to do the same. "Come on, we might as well eat some of this while we're waiting for Gage and Kayla to get here, and while Nanette tells us what's going on."

Nanette had picked up a dish towel to dry a plate, but she put the plate away without drying it, then tossed the towel on the counter. "It'd be better if we wait until Gage and Kayla are here, because I don't know the whole story," she hedged, then peered out the kitchen window as though she could magically make Gage's Dodge Ram appear outside.

"They can tell us the details when they get here," Tristan said, taking a bite of sandwich, then nodding his approval as he swallowed. "Good po'boy." He glanced at Chantelle. "I know you're hungry. You should eat."

She knew he wasn't any more interested in eating than she was, knowing that Nanette, Gage and Kayla were about to shed some light on her ghost problem, but she was also smart enough to know that she and Tristan needed to be at their strongest if they had to encounter her ghost again. So she picked up the sandwich and took a big bite. He was right; it was delicious. Fried shrimp, with just the right amount of Cajun seasoning, crisp lettuce, mayonnaise and tomato all combined on the toasted French bread to produce a great po'boy. In fact, Nanette's sandwich ranked second in the high points of this day, right beneath the multiple orgasms Tristan had given her earlier.

She stifled a laugh, and Tristan's eyes crinkled at the corners. "Thinking about this morning?" he asked quietly, and she nodded, then took another bite.

Nanette took advantage of their interaction to turn her back to them and dry some dishes, but Tristan still wasn't letting her off that easily.

"Over here, Nan. Tell us what's going on." He tapped the spot beside him, and though she glared at him as she did so, Nanette dropped the towel again and moved to the table.

"Gage didn't tell me anything specific."

"But he told you enough to make you nearly bang my bedroom door down and enough for you to prepare food as though we were on death row and this was our last meal."

Nanette's eyes practically bugged out at that, and Tristan shook his head. "Hell, Nanette, that's not what I meant. I'm not going anywhere and neither is Chantelle. The only one who'll make a permanent exit, the way I see it, is that ghost. But we can't make that happen if we don't know everything there is to know about him. What aren't you telling me?"

He'd totally forgotten about his sandwich now and pushed the plate away while he waited for Nan's answer. Chantelle did the same. She'd had a couple of bites, and that was enough. Her stomach couldn't handle food right now, anyway. Did Nan know something that would help them send her ghost away faster? Or—and this was more likely from the worried creases on her forehead—did she know for sure that he would return?

"Please, Nanette, tell us," she begged.

Nan looked from Tristan to Chantelle. Her mouth twitched downward at one corner and her head shook slightly as she spoke. "Gage said Kayla has figured out who the ghost is. Or rather, who he was."

Chantelle's heart pounded so hard she could swear she heard it. "Kayla knows him? Knew him?" What did that mean? If the ghost had come because of Chantelle's book, how would Kayla know him? But if Kayla *did* know him, then chances were, so did Chantelle. The two of them had been together for most of their lives. They'd become as close as sisters at the orphanage and had stayed close after their abuse, the trial and Lillian's murder. And because of their past, their acquaintances were few.

Her breathing quickened. She'd thought that perhaps this ghost had targeted her because of her book; she'd thought that he'd believed she knew something about helping him leave the middle realm, since that was the premise of her fictional story. But what if the reason this ghost targeted her had nothing at all to do with her book—and everything to do with her past?

Chantelle turned from Nanette to Tristan. "He knew. He knew *exactly* how the knife had been held on me back then, and that's the way he placed it against my throat last night. He *knows* me. And I know him, don't I?"

The back door banged against the wall as Gage opened it and he and Kayla rushed in.

"Chantelle." Kayla's face was pale, her eyes and hair appearing even darker than usual due to her pallor. Clutching a wadded envelope, she moved to the table and scooted a chair close to her friend.

"What is it, Kayla?" Chantelle's pulse intensified. How had Kayla figured out who he was?

"I have something to tell you, something to show you," she said urgently.

"Who is he?" Chantelle asked.

Kayla glanced at Nanette, but she didn't appear upset. She'd obviously known it would be impossible for Nan not to say *something* about what Kayla had learned about the ghost. "How many days has it been since the ghost first came to your apartment? Do you know when, exactly, he showed up? What day?"

Gage stood directly behind his wife and placed his hands on her shoulders as though she also needed support. Why? Chantelle wondered. How did this ghost know Kayla?

"How many days?" Kayla repeated.

Chantelle blinked, then thought back to when the radio in her apartment had first started blaring that song and when she'd first felt that bone-chilling cold that denoted his unwanted presence. "Five days ago."

"Tuesday," Gage said, then looked at Kayla. "That's when you had that nightmare." He shook his head. "Hell, we thought it was just a bad dream."

"What nightmare?" Nanette asked.

"Kayla dreamed someone was holding something against her neck trying to strangle her. She started screaming, and I woke up and held her, told her I was there and wouldn't let anything hurt her."

"I was remembering the past, those nights they'd come take us out of our rooms at the orphanage," Kayla said, her expression grave as she recalled the horrors of their past. "Everything they did. I haven't had one of those nightmares since Gage and I married, so I was shocked to be having one, and I couldn't figure out what caused it. But once I realized that Gage was with me, and that there was no way he'd let anyone hurt me, the nightmare stopped completely."

"But now you don't think it was just a nightmare, do you?" Nan prompted.

"No. I think he was there. Chantelle's ghost was there, and when he saw that I wasn't afraid, he left."

"When you conquered your fear of the ghost, he went away," Tristan said, looking at Chantelle, then back at Kayla. "You think Chantelle's ghost came after you first, and when he knew you weren't afraid, he went to Chantelle?"

Kayla nodded. "I'm sorry I didn't think of it sooner, or I'd have at least mentioned the dream. But there was so much going on around here, and I really did think it was just a nightmare."

"But now you think it was my ghost?" Chantelle leaned forward. "Why, Kayla? Who do you think he is?"

Kayla's mouth thinned as she pulled a wrinkled letter from the envelope. "Gage and I got our mail from the box yesterday afternoon, but we didn't get around to opening it until today. I wish I hadn't waited, but I had no idea." Her fingers trembled as she unfolded the page. "Your name is also on here, so I'm sure they sent a copy to you, too. I guess it's at your apartment. They're required, you know, to tell us when something happens."

Though her statements would be confusing to anyone who hadn't shared their past, Chantelle knew exactly what Kayla was talking about. "They" referred to the State of Louisiana, and the fact that the state was required to tell victims who'd testified against a criminal if something happened regarding that criminal while in prison. If a prisoner was transferred or paroled or escaped, the victims would be notified. Wayne Romero had been murdered in prison a year ago, so Chantelle knew that wasn't the prisoner Kayla referred to. But his son, Aidan Dominic, was in prison now for attempting to kill Kayla—and for Lillian's murder.

"A.D.?" she asked. "A.D. has something to do with my ghost?"

"I didn't want to believe it," Kayla said, and Tristan instinctively moved closer to Chantelle. "But I do."

"Tell me, Kayla."

"He hung himself," Kayla told her. "In prison. Five days ago."

Chantelle's mind reeled. A. D. Romero had hung himself in prison? She suddenly believed it without a doubt, because A.D.'s death five days ago would put every horrendous piece of the puzzle into place.

Her ghost was A. D. Romero.

He'd gone after Kayla first, but Gage had already helped her conquer her fear. So Romero had no power over her. But that wasn't the case for Chantelle. She had so much fear that he'd only grown stronger in her presence. Damn him.

A. D. Romero had haunted her apartment, locked her in her car, and pushed her foot to the accelerator of her Beetle. *A.D.* had thrown that rock through Tristan's windshield, and *A.D.* had held that knife to her throat— the same way he'd done so many years ago when he and his father abused her repeatedly.

She hated him, and she hated that he was terrorizing her again, even after his death.

Tristan draped his arm protectively around her. "Chantelle, I won't let him hurt you, I swear it."

She focused on him, on the conviction in his voice. He thought she was scared, but she wasn't, not anymore. She was too damn livid to be scared. If she had to conquer her fears to send A.D where he belonged, she would.

"You can help me," she said, finding more strength with every word and, oddly, feeling Lillian's presence around her, as well, as though Lillian's arms circled her now as much as Tristan's. "You all can *help* me, but it's up to me to send him away, like Adeline said. And I will. I'm *not* going to let him win, not this time, not again." Then she swallowed and added, "Lillian, I promise you, he will pay for what he did to you, and for what he did to me."

She knew that Nanette, Tristan, Kayla, Gage—and all of the Vicknairs—would do anything to help her accomplish her goal, but she also knew the truth. It wasn't up to Tristan or his family to send A. D. Romero to hell.

It was up to her.

15

TRISTAN HAD KNOWN she could be stubborn and determined, particularly when it came to protecting those she cared about, but Chantelle was even stronger than he'd realized. She lifted a knife from the block and held it in her hand, her fingers clasping the handle as she turned her wrist to better examine the blade.

Kayla stood nearby, a cutting board in front of her and a bulging yellow onion waiting for her attention. But she wasn't concerned with what was in front of her; she was concerned about her friend. "You sure?" she questioned for the third time, as Chantelle continued staring at the knife in her hand. She also had a cutting board in front of her with a bell pepper on it. When she'd insisted she wanted to help Nanette prepare the meal and tackle her fear of knives on her own, they'd all been hesitant, but they'd known better than to tell her no.

Tristan was having an especially hard time watching her, knowing how difficult the simple task of chopping peppers was for a woman who'd been raped with a knife held to her throat. He'd been standing a few feet away, close enough, he thought, to defend her if A. D. Romero returned, but he moved closer; he couldn't help it. Watching the color drain from her face and seeing the pulse quicken at her throat was simply too much to bear. He couldn't stand the thought of her going through this alone.

She was so intent on moving the knife to the green pepper that she didn't even notice Tristan was right next to her now. Not wanting anything to obstruct her view, he eased her blond curls behind her shoulders. She didn't even look up, but remained riveted to the knife in her hand. She clutched it so fiercely that her knuckles were colorless, and Tristan had no doubt she was battling for control.

"Let me help you with the first cut," he said. "And then you can try on your own, okay?" He knew it wasn't what she wanted. She wanted to battle this fear head-on, but every tense movement of her body told him she wasn't ready, not yet. Not without him. "Chantelle, let me help," he repeated softly, wrapping his palm around the hand holding the knife.

She swallowed, looked up at him as though just realizing he was there, and nodded. "The first cut," she said, allowing that much, and Tristan knew better than to ask for more.

He moved behind her and circled his other arm around her to help her hold the pepper steady as, together, they brought the knife closer to the side of the vegetable, and then sliced the top away.

She relaxed slightly when the first cut was completed, and Tristan leaned his face close to hers, then gently kissed her cheek. "You did it."

"*We* did it," she corrected, but she didn't sound disappointed. She sounded confident. "Thank you."

"No problem."

"I need to try this on my own now," she said without missing a beat, and Tristan nodded.

"I know. But you'll tell me…"

"If I feel anything at all, I'll tell you."

Gage entered the kitchen. "I started loading the siding into my truck, but I wanted to check on things in here," he said, slapping his hands together as he moved toward Kayla. He glanced at Chantelle and the knife in her hand. "How's it going?" He'd purposely left the kitchen when Nanette suggested they start cooking, because he hadn't thought Chantelle needed more of an audience as she fought her inner demons. Now, obviously, curiosity had gotten the best of him, because he eyed Chantelle, Kayla, Nanette and Tristan as though silently willing somebody to tell him what had happened.

Nanette stopped sautéeing green onions on the stove, also apparently deciding to forgo any pretense of paying attention to anything in the room but what Chantelle was doing. All eyes were on her, yet she was so focused on her task she didn't notice.

"Lillian." Chantelle barely whispered her sister's name, but Tristan heard. He didn't speak, didn't acknowledge that he'd heard the name or that he wondered whether Lillian's spirit was with her now, helping her. She took another breath, then whispered, "Tristan."

He started to respond, but then she repeated her sister's name and Tristan realized she wasn't talking to Lillian now, and she wasn't talking to him, either. She was gaining her strength to conquer this fear by keeping her mind on the people that mattered the most to her, and those people were her sister and Tristan.

His heart swelled with admiration. And love.

She eased her hand down the pepper and continued slicing it, each cut produced with more ease than the one before.

"Chantelle, you're okay?" Kayla asked.

"I'm fine," she said, turning to glance at Tristan as she spoke. "Really."

EVENTUALLY, CHANTELLE CONVINCED Tristan that she was okay in the kitchen with Nanette and Kayla, and that he could help Gage load the pile of debris outside. She'd spent the entire afternoon cooking with Nanette and Kayla and was almost comfortable with the knife now. Today, thanks to Tristan, she'd crossed two of her fears off the list. She'd achieved not one, but several climaxes that had her body burning with desire and still aching for more. She'd have that—*more*—with him tonight, and she couldn't wait. And Tristan had also helped her with the knives. He'd *known* when her fear had started to creep in, when she first held that knife in her hand, and he'd placed his body against hers, his hand over hers and had given her the strength she needed to face the fear and continue. It was the same thing he'd done last night, when he'd held his own desires at bay as they'd bathed each other. He'd wanted her, the evidence of that was undeniable, but he had let her have control and take her time becoming used to the two of them together. And then, when he'd touched her, kissed her, loved her, she'd thought of nothing and no one but him. Yet still, *he* hadn't been satisfied sexually.

But he would be. And Chantelle truly looked forward to making it happen.

"Is this yours?" Nanette asked, holding up the pad where Tristan and Chantelle had listed her fears.

Chantelle nodded.

Kayla moved toward Nan to see what was written on the page, then she read the list aloud. "Knives, intimacy and being alone. Those are your fears." She glanced at Chantelle. "You're okay with knives now, right?"

"They're not my favorite," Chantelle admitted, "but I'm not totally afraid of them anymore, and he didn't return today when I used this knife, so I guess I've got that one covered."

"Thank goodness," Kayla said. "And...intimacy?"

"I'd say she handled that one last night and this morning." One of Nanette's dark brows arched upward as though daring Chantelle to deny what she and Tristan had shared.

"I did, though we're not done with that one yet." She couldn't hold back a smile.

"O-kay," Nan said, in a that's-probably-enough-about-that-subject tone. Then she looked at the last item on the list. "There's only one more, then."

Chantelle could have told her that there were actually two more, the one listed and the one she'd felt awkward sharing with Tristan, but she kept that to herself for now.

"Being alone," Kayla said. "Based on how long it took you to convince Tristan to leave you here with us while he helped Gage outside, I'm betting he isn't too keen on letting you tackle that one."

"He isn't, but truthfully, I haven't been ready to deal with it yet, either."

"You think when you're alone again, the past will come back to haunt you?" Nanette asked.

"That A.D. will come back to haunt you?" Kayla clarified.

"I want to believe that he won't. Honestly, I feel like he can't touch me anymore, and as long as I'm with all of you, or even near to just Tristan, I believe it's true. But I really haven't tested being alone yet."

The door from the hallway swung open, and Jenee, her eyes swollen and her hair on top of her head in a wild ponytail that was obviously the result of a fitful bout of sleep, entered the kitchen. "What time is it?" she asked, squinting at the old round clock on one wall.

"Nearly six," Nanette answered. "I thought you were volunteering at the homeless shelter today."

"I did, but then I came home. Needed to sleep," she explained, still apparently trying to wake up. "Six at night?" She crossed to the refrigerator and withdrew a pitcher of tea, then poured a glass.

"Yes," Nanette answered. "Are you okay?"

"I have a…ghost coming," she said.

Chantelle recalled hearing that Jenee's assignments often first visited her in dreams. She started to ask Jenee about this particular ghost, but then Jenee stopped drinking her tea and eyed Chantelle.

"Oh, I was so wrapped up in him—this ghost," she said, "that I forgot completely about the one haunting you. Did anything else happen after you wrecked your car?" She shook her head, then touched the messy ponytail as several stray strands poked her in the eye. "My ghost really has taken over my day," she muttered. "Sorry I forgot about yours."

"It's okay," Chantelle replied, then went on to relay everything that had happened.

Clearly shocked, Jenee quickly came to full alert. "Oh, man, I should have stayed awake to help."

"You aren't able to stay awake when you've got an assignment coming," Nan pointed out. "And there wasn't anything you could've done that we couldn't accomplish on our own. It's just good that Tristan was here last night when A.D. tried to attack Chantelle in the kitchen."

"My brother will protect you any way he can," Jenee said, reminding Chantelle that she was not only a Vicknair, but Tristan's sister.

"I know he will." Chantelle was more certain of that than anything.

"You take care of your ghost, and we'll help Chantelle take care of hers," Nan said.

"My ghost is gone for now." Jenee sounded a bit disappointed.

"What does that mean? That he isn't crossing, after all?" Chantelle asked, always curious about how the mediums handled their spirits, both because of her writing and because Lillian had needed a medium in order to cross over.

"I hope that isn't what it means," Jenee said, then added, "I haven't helped him find the light yet, and I haven't officially received him as an assignment. Nothing has shown on the tea service." She shrugged. "He's different from every other assignment I've had."

Nanette, Kayla and Chantelle waited for Jenee to explain further, but instead, she took another swallow of tea before saying, "Listen, my ghost will obviously keep. He isn't here now. Yours, however, is a different matter. What can I do to help?"

"I don't think there's anything you can do right now," Chantelle said. "I have one more fear on the list to conquer, and I'm not all that certain I'm able to do it yet."

"Chantelle is afraid of being alone," Kayla explained. "And she's already tackled her other fears today. We're thinking that she may need to wait and try the biggee tomorrow, or whenever she feels she's ready."

"I don't want to wait any longer than tomorrow," Chantelle declared.

"No doubt tomorrow will be a big day for everyone, then," Nanette said. "Charles Roussel and his committee are supposed to come early in the morning, before I leave for work, to do the inspection."

"We're ready for it, aren't we?" Jenee asked. "We just have to show that we're making progress toward the renovations, and we are, right?"

"Yeah, we've actually done more than we'd told them we'd do, so there shouldn't be anything he can do but give us the go-ahead to continue. However, knowing Roussel, he'll do his best to find *some*thing wrong and stop us from getting any money from the River Road Historical Society." She frowned. "I wish we would hear something from the National Register. If *they* gave us the thumbs-up, there wouldn't be anything at all he could say about it."

"You haven't heard from them yet?"

"No, I submitted the proposal six months ago, but they're really backed up with other homes and plantations trying to obtain that status. We won't have their seal of approval for this inspection, but maybe next time we will. And then I can tell Roussel to leave us alone for good."

"Oh, I forgot all about helping you cook for the firehouse," Jenee said apologetically, lifting the lid on the pot to examine the simmering gumbo.

"No problem. You were dealing with a ghost, and we all know that takes priority. Besides, Kayla and Chantelle helped. You can bring it with me to the fire station if you want, though. We should probably take it on over there now."

"Sure."

"You two want to come with us?" Nan asked as she turned off the stove, then grabbed the pot handles to carry it out.

"I'll stay here with Gage," Kayla said. "And I know Chantelle doesn't need to leave right now, just in case." She didn't have to complete the sentence, but they all knew what had been implied: *in case A.D. returns.*

Chantelle knew she hadn't completed everything required to send the ghost on his way, so she agreed with Kayla. "Yeah, I'll stay here."

Kayla opened the back door for Nan to carry the pot through, with Jenee following closely. "I'll get the car door," she called to Nanette as they exited. "We'll be back in a little bit," she said, and then Kayla and Chantelle were the only two in the kitchen.

"Why don't we do the dishes while we're waiting for the guys to come back in?" Kayla moved toward the sink.

Chantelle agreed and followed her, then mechanically rinsed and dried the dishes as Kayla washed them. She'd wanted the chance to talk to her friend in private, and she wasn't going to miss the opportunity to ask the question that had bothered her ever since she learned that A. D. Romero had hung himself in prison.

"Kayla, how did you conquer your fears so completely? And why do mine seem to be so much tougher for me to deal with?"

"Gage and I discussed that this morning after we got that letter from the state," Kayla said, her hands submerged in the sudsy water and busily scrubbing a stubborn pot as she spoke. "The only thing we could come up with is that I'm truly not afraid anymore. Like I said earlier, Gage was there when A.D. tried to come after me in my sleep, and A.D. couldn't touch me with Gage giving me strength. It did take a long time to get over those fears, to stop being afraid to close my eyes at night. I never knew when I'd start to sleep and then find Wayne and A.D. there, taking control of my dreams, except it wasn't really a dream—it was a memory. All of those horrible memories of them taking each of us from our room, and of the things they did to us when they had us alone—I didn't know if I'd ever get past all the pain, but with Gage's help, I did. And I'm not afraid anymore."

"But I am," Chantelle admitted softly. "And that's why he has power over me and no power over you."

"You haven't had anyone to help you get past it. I have Gage, and Shelby has Phillip," Kayla said, reminding Chantelle of their other friend who'd also endured A.D. and Wayne Romero's torture.

"You have Tristan now," Kayla continued, "and all the other Vicknairs, too, including Gage and me, to help you. Dealing with the kind of past we endured is something that doesn't happen on your own, Chantelle. I couldn't do it alone, and neither could Shelby. It just took you a little longer to find the right people, the right person, to help you accomplish that goal. But you've found them now, the Vicknairs. *And* you've found Tristan." She withdrew her left hand from the soapy water and held it up while the bubbles dripped back into the sink, her diamond glinted. "There's nothing like finding the right man," she whispered, "except for, perhaps, finding out that you're going to make him a father."

Chantelle nearly dropped the dish in her hand, but she managed to place it on the counter. "Are you serious?"

"I haven't told anyone yet, not even Gage, because I haven't even taken a home pregnancy test yet, but all the signs are there. I'm late, and I'm often tired, and I've been queasy the past few mornings." The back door opened, and Gage and Tristan loudly made their entrance, while Kayla whispered, "Not a word yet. I'm going to tell him after I've taken the test."

Chantelle's excitement at Kayla's news bubbled within her, but she'd keep the secret until Kayla was ready to share. She silently prayed that one day she would find the contentment, the happiness, that Kayla had found with Gage and that Shelby had found with Phillip. It *was* possible to move beyond the pain of their past, and if her friends had been able to do it, then she would, too. But as Kayla said, she wouldn't be able to do it alone. She didn't have to, anyway, not when Tristan had shown her time and time again that he was as determined as Chantelle to help her overcome her past. And unless she'd read him wrong, he was also determined to be a part of her future.

"Everything okay?" he asked, stepping close to her and gently running the backs of his fingers down her cheek.

Chantelle glanced at Gage kissing Kayla, and she reveled in the joy of finding that same intimacy with a man, this man. "Everything's nearly perfect."

"Nearly?"

She brought her mouth to his ear. "Everything will be perfect when you're deep inside me."

Tristan's jaw nudged her cheek as he smiled his agreement. "Can't think of anywhere I'd rather be."

16

CHANTELLE INHALED the warm night air and watched as Tristan carried a surplus of tools to the shed. Since the primary entrance to the shed was still covered in debris from her crash, he used the smaller door in back to stow the tools before Roussel's visit tomorrow morning. He and Gage had loaded siding until well past dark, and then Tristan had continued cleaning up while Gage hauled the debris away. Obviously he wanted the place to look as good as possible for the inspection. Chantelle truly admired his dedication to his family and their beloved home.

It'd been at least an hour since Gage had returned, picked up Kayla and went home. Nanette and Jenee had also called it a night and gone to bed, Nanette because she was exhausted and Jenee because she said her ghost was beckoning her to dream again. Only Chantelle and Tristan remained.

She gathered several hammers and a toolbelt that one of Tristan's firemen had left hanging on the side of a ladder and carried them to the shed, where Tristan took them from her and put them away. The mere brush of his fingers against her palms stirred her desire again. She wanted him, and the heat in his green eyes, looking at her every so often as they moved about the yard and put the tools away, said he wanted her just as much.

His biceps flexed steadily as he climbed a tall ladder, still propped against the side of the house. He wore old jeans that rested low on his hips as he moved up the ladder. The need within Chantelle increased exponentially as she stood mesmerized by the man. He was at such ease perched on a high rung, and she realized that while she knew plenty about his ability to communicate with the dead, she knew virtually nothing about his occupation and about what had first made him decide to climb ladders like that one and take on raging fires on a regular basis.

"Tristan." She spoke loudly, since he was near the roof now, grabbing hammers and other tools the men had left on the roof's edge.

Without hesitation, he climbed down the ladder with the tools in hand and moved instinctively toward her. "You okay? You don't feel him again, do you?"

"No," she said, touched by his concern. "But I realized I've never asked you what made you become a firefighter. And how do you do it day in and day out without fear? You aren't scared, are you?"

"Of fire?" he asked, as the two of them crossed the yard toward the shed. A full moon provided their only source of light, but it was bright enough to illuminate the tiny building through the opened door. Tristan put the last of the tools inside, then turned back to Chantelle. "I'm not scared when it's obvious I'm in control." He wiped his brow with the back of his hand, pushing his dark hair to the side with the motion and drawing more attention to those green eyes, lit by the glowing moon. "But I'd be lying if I said I'm not more than a little scared when I'm face-to-face with a fire I can't control."

Chantelle thought of him in that very situation, approaching a building engulfed in flame and knowing that it was up to him to confront the fire head-on. She couldn't stand the thought of him in danger, yet she knew Tristan well enough to know that he wouldn't back down from that situation, or from any other. She'd seen that firsthand when he confronted A.D.'s spirit and as he helped her do the same. "How do you do it? Face the fear?" She was asking from more than mere curiosity; she was going to have to face the fear of being alone and potentially having A. D. Romero try to attack her again without Tristan there to help. Maybe if she knew how Tristan faced those fires, she could figure out a plan of action for being completely on her own.

He leaned against the side of the shed, stuffed his hands into his pockets and thought about his answer before speaking. Chantelle took the opportunity to survey the incredible image before her—Tristan Vicknair, his body glistening with a slight sheen of sweat from his labor, and his jeans riding even lower with his hands in those pockets. He looked extremely…male.

"I know why you're asking, and I'm not sure if my answer will give you what you will need when we do try to tackle the last fear on your list, but the truth is, I confront the fire because I never know…" He paused.

"Never know what?" she asked, concentrating on his response, because her mind had been momentarily sidetracked.

"Whether my fear may cost someone their life. Sometimes firefighters know when people are trapped inside. Sometimes we don't. But we can never assume that just because we don't know for sure that there's a victim trapped in a burning building that there isn't one. I have to face the fear, or I risk living the rest of my life wondering if I could have saved someone else's."

She swallowed, her feelings toward him magnified by his honest response and by his endless ability to put others' lives before his own. Then again, that was simply the way he was made, the very substance of him, and it was part of what made her so enamored with him, so captivated by being with him and by the thought of being one with him. Yes, she was drawn to him physically, but he'd also captured her emotionally, as well.

"I don't know if that was the answer you were looking for to help you with what you've got to do," he said.

Even now, he was wondering if he was satisfying her needs, giving her what she needed to confront A.D. on her own. "That's exactly what I wanted to know." She did know what she'd do. It'd worked earlier today, when she'd used that knife in the kitchen. She'd thought of the people who mattered most to her, Lillian and Tristan, and realized that she was willing to confront any fear for them; she didn't want Lillian to have died in vain, and she didn't want to lose the chance to live, truly live, with Tristan. *That* was what helped her today, and *that* was what would help her when she faced A.D. on her own.

"You care to explain that?" he asked.

But she didn't want to talk about A.D. now. In fact,

she didn't want to talk at all. What she wanted…was the man beside her. "Just know that I have an idea of what I'll do if he shows up again, but right now I have something else I want to do."

She reached for his hand. "I want to make love in the moonlight."

His eyes glowed, and it had nothing to do with the moonlight. "Here?"

"You have a problem with that?" she asked, growing more excited at the thought of the two of them, together, outside.

"Hell, no."

Before Chantelle had time to process what he was doing, he wrapped his arms around her and picked her up, her legs instantly straddling him as he walked away from the shed. Her jean shorts rubbed against her sensitive center with every step. She'd been ultrasensitive all day, partially because her body was still highly stimulated from the multitude of orgasms that had started her day, and partially because she still hadn't been sated deep inside, where she wanted Tristan the most.

He kissed her as they moved. Chantelle ran her fingers through his hair and enjoyed the way the strands tickled her palms, and the way his talented mouth caressed hers, teasing her tongue with strokes that mimicked what their bodies would be doing—soon.

Cool metal met the back of her legs as he placed her on the tailgate of Gerry's truck, and she laughed against his mouth when she realized where they were, and where their first time would be—on the back of a pickup that had seen better days. Undoubtedly he'd thought the pickup would be more conducive to what they were doing than the hood of his Jeep. He was probably right.

Tristan apparently guessed why she was laughing, and he broke the kiss and grinned at her. "Changed your mind? Want to wait until we've got a nice soft bed?"

"Do you want to wait?" she countered.

"Hell, no," he said, repeating his earlier statement with a to-die-for smile.

"Me, neither." She crossed her arms in front of her, grabbed the hem of her navy T-shirt and pulled it over her head. Then she tossed it to the side, while Tristan ran a finger along the lacy edge of her navy bra.

"You always match, don't you?" he asked. "The other day, when you wore the pink top, you wore pink underwear. When you wear navy, you've got navy underneath. Is it that way for every color?"

She nodded. "Always."

"Yet another secret method for maintaining control, isn't it?" he asked, and she was thrown by how well he knew her already.

"Yeah."

His mouth flattened, and he looked from the lacy bra to her face, then focused on her eyes. "I hate it that those things happened to you back then, hate it that you'd never experienced real pleasure until last night. And I hate it that you had to find your own ways of obtaining control." He eased his face closer to hers, then softly kissed her as he unfastened the front closure on her bra and tenderly slid his hands over her breasts. "But I'm glad you found ways to have the control you needed, and I'm very glad you learned how to find pleasure—with me."

He moved his tongue across her lower lip, and Chantelle opened her mouth for his thorough perusal. He tasted so good, felt so right, as he kissed her softly. His hands caressed her as he removed her bra, her shorts, her panties, and then massaged her intimately.

She was completely naked before Tristan had removed the first item of his clothing. "I want you," she said, and attempted to pull his shirt over his head. His body was hot from exertion, or perhaps from what they were doing, and it was no small feat to pull the fabric from all of those overheated muscles, but she managed.

Smiling, he unfastened his jeans and within moments was as naked as she, his penis hard and long and very near where she wanted it. He'd withdrawn a foil packet from his pocket, and he tore it open, then sheathed his erection while she watched, mesmerized by the way his hands moved over his length.

She shifted her hips forward, spreading her legs more to allow better access, then looked into those green eyes, still visible due to the light from the moon, and still driving her mad with desire. "Please."

He entered her slowly, and Chantelle was grateful for his gentle patience. She wasn't as ready as she'd thought, and she wasn't sure whether she could handle all of him. She knew he'd barely pushed inside, and she was already tensing against his girth, her body betraying her and what she knew she wanted, needed.

"Chantelle, we don't have to," he said, his voice strained from his attempt to keep his desire in check, but Chantelle didn't want him to stop.

"I don't know what's wrong," she said honestly.

He gently eased her away from him, so that his erection wasn't even near her center.

"Tristan, no, please don't stop. I want to."

"I know you do, *chère,* but I also know that I haven't done my part to get you ready, and that's my own damn fault for wanting you so much I'm rushing." He leaned over her, until Chantelle's back was flush against the bed of the truck. "I'm going to do this right, and before we do *that,* you're going to come."

Then he kissed her neck, gently nipping at the curve between her neck and shoulder before continuing down her chest. Chantelle closed her eyes, felt the warmth of the Louisiana night and more than that, felt the heat of Tristan's kisses along her body, as he slowly moved from one breast to the other, tenderly caressing her nipples with his tongue. She moaned her contentment, then gasped when he made his way along her abdomen, still kissing, nipping, sucking. Her legs opened and her hips lifted from the truck bed, and then she felt him move her to the edge of the tailgate, her legs opened for him and her body on fire.

Chantelle held her breath as Tristan magically used his tongue against her clitoris, kissing her, sucking her, nibbling her until she was so close that she could feel the impending orgasm pressing, pushing, yearning to be set free. Amazing that she'd gone so many years without being able to let her body go, because now that Tristan had gained her trust, taught her to truly find pleasure with him, she couldn't get enough.

"Tristan," she pleaded, needing that release.

His mouth left her, and she felt his hardened length

against her burning center—now hot, wet and ready to have him give her…everything.

"Please," she repeated. "Now, Tristan, please."

He pushed inside her, and this time, he slid in deep, and she immediately convulsed around him, her hips lifting to bring him farther in. She'd been hovering on the brink of climax, and the magnitude of the moment, of joining completely with a man—not out of force, but out of true desire—set all her emotions free. Her body was his. Her mind, her soul *and* her heart, completely his. She had no fear of this, had no fear of him. She only had love.

Her climax rippled through her core, while tears of pleasure, of triumph, and of surrender trickled freely down her cheeks.

She loved him, loved Tristan Vicknair with every fiber of her being. She—*loved*—him.

17

TRISTAN WASN'T EXACTLY a bedroom-and-bedroom-only kind of guy when it came to sex. On the contrary, he'd had his share of sex in unique locations. In one night with Chantelle, however, he could honestly say he'd topped every prior scenario, both in originality and satisfaction. Originality, because the two of them had made love in every possible location surrounding the plantation house, starting with Gerry's truck, then a rocker on the front porch, then against the side of the house and finally—wildly—on the cane harvester in the shed. When at last they'd made it into the house, they were thoroughly exhausted. But that didn't keep them from two additional encounters through the night, when Chantelle's soft, curvy body had nuzzled him in sleep, and his cock had responded as though he hadn't had sex in years.

He'd known that making love again with Chantelle would be incredible when she finally allowed her body to let go and enjoy the pleasure of sex, but he'd been surprised with how adventurous she was, willing to try everything, wanting to experience everything. There was no way she wasn't sore, not because Tristan had been rough with her, but because she pushed him not to hold back. In fact, she seemed even more excited when she sensed his own loss of control.

She snuggled against him, blond curls tumbling around her as she slept, and his penis responded accordingly, totally in sync with the beautiful naked woman in the bed. She smiled softly and pried her eyes open to peer up at him. "No more fear."

Her comment, unfortunately, reminded him of the most pressing matter at hand, and it wasn't his dick pressing against her side. Obviously she'd mastered her fear of intimacy, and yesterday, she'd conquered her fear of knives. Two things off the short list, but the last one...

"I can do it." Her sky-blue eyes were serious now, sobered by the same realization he had—that she really needed to conquer her last fear and send A. D. Romero away for good. "I want you to leave me here today and let me face being alone." She smiled reassuringly. "After last night, I feel like I could take on the world, and that includes a troublesome ghost."

Tristan wanted to point out that *troublesome* wasn't nearly a strong-enough adjective, but perhaps she was downplaying A.D.'s viciousness to give her the courage she needed. Tristan wasn't about to stifle that.

"However..." She kissed his neck, snuggled closer.

"However?"

"Another orgasm or two might help."

He laughed. "I can't imagine how, but I'm not about to argue with you."

"Maybe it's because I went so long without having them, and maybe it's because the entire amazing process is still so new to me, but after I have one, I feel like there's nothing in the world I can't do."

Tristan couldn't deny the pride that surged potently through him and caused his cock to kick up a notch. So, the orgasms he'd given her made her feel she could do anything. Not bad for a guy's ego. He was also glad she didn't seem afraid of being alone and facing that final hurdle—as long as she had an orgasm or two before she did.

"So," she said, giving him a sultry smile, "are you going to give me what I need?"

Tristan didn't get a chance to answer. Voices in an escalating heated confrontation came from outside and commanded their attention.

"What's going on?" Chantelle asked, as he left the bed and made his way to the window.

He immediately saw Nanette, standing beside Charles Roussel's black Mercedes with her hands on her hips and her shoulders squared. Roussel casually leaned against the door of his car and had the audacity to grin at Tristan's cousin. Even from his heightened vantage, Tristan could tell that the guy's grin was pissing Nanette off more, and he could also tell that Roussel was thoroughly enjoying getting a rise out of her. His smile was almost as broad as the one he'd displayed on his campaign posters.

"Who is it?" Chantelle asked.

"Nanette and Roussel," he answered, then cracked the window open so he could hear a bit of the conversation and try to figure out what had Nanette so worked up.

"They gave us two months before the next inspection," Nanette said. "So there's no need in you dropping by Saturday or any other time to check on our progress.

We're doing everything the committee asked us to do. The temporary supports are holding up fine while we're preparing for the structural repairs, and Ryan has already lined up a bunch of his construction friends to help us out every weekend for the next eight weeks. They may even finish the job before the committee returns."

"Your house is no longer stable, Nanette. The entire right side was pushed in from Katrina, and even if the foundation seems adequate, the actual structure is another story," Charles replied smoothly. Unlike Nan's, his voice was hardly raised at all, which seemed to infuriate her even more.

"Which is why we've got those men to help with repairs," she shot back.

"Like the committee members said, that's a big job you're looking at. I hardly think a few men working one day a week is going to do the trick, do you?"

"We're not attempting to do everything on our own. We're merely getting the job started while we wait for the historical society to approve the house for funding and repairs. And, as the committee members agreed this morning, we're on the right track. Not one of them said anything about demolition."

"I believe I heard it mentioned," he said.

"By you!"

Roussel withdrew his hand from the pocket of his expensive slacks and checked his equally expensive watch as though bored with this discussion. But the smile on his face said he wasn't bored; he was enjoying every minute of it. "Aren't you due in class, Ms. Vicknair? I do recall you work at the local high school, don't you?"

"You know damn well where I work," she snapped. "And you knew I'd have to call in a substitute teacher to handle my class this morning when you and your committee got here late. But I *am* going in to relieve her, and I do need to get going. So if you don't mind, I'd appreciate it if you'd go to—" She paused, sneering at him. "I mean, I'd appreciate it if you'd go."

"Happy to," he said. "But I don't think I'll go all that far. I haven't visited with my brother in a while." Roussel's brother, Johnny, owned the plantation next to the Vicknairs', a fact that Nanette despised, since it gave the parish president even more opportunity to check on their progress. "Then again, I could wait and visit him on Saturday, when I come back out here."

"Don't even think about it," she warned. "We'll be busy working, and I don't need you coming out here and distracting us."

"Am I that much of a distraction to you, Nanette?" He stepped closer to her with every word. "Keep your mind off your work, do I?"

Tristan watched this last interaction with more than a little interest. He'd often suspected there was more to their constant feuding than met the eye, but Nanette had never confirmed that she and Roussel had a history. Now, though, from the way his cousin took a small step away from the guy, he again wondered.

"Don't flatter yourself," she said, then turned briskly enough to send her black hair swinging.

"It's only flattery if it isn't true," he said smugly, then climbed in his car and drove away before Nanette had a chance for a rebuttal.

The entire house rattled when she slammed the door

and then stomped up the stairs. Tristan moved back to the bed and climbed in, or he suspected he'd be giving Nanette a look at his goods in about three seconds.

Chantelle held the sheet up as he climbed in and had apparently heard Nanette and Roussel's interaction, as well. "He really knows how to push her buttons, doesn't he?" she asked.

"I'll say."

"Sounds like she's headed this way. Do you need to unlock the—"

Chantelle didn't finish the question, and Tristan didn't bother answering. There was no need. Nanette had already entered their room and stood in the doorway, her face red, her eyes narrowed and her chest heaving.

"I don't suppose you're here to bring me coffee in bed," Tristan said.

"He infuriates me!" Nan announced.

"We heard. But I gather the inspection went okay, from the sound of things?" Tristan asked.

She took a deep calming breath and leaned against the doorway. "Yeah, it went great, but it'd have been better if that asshole had left with the rest of the committee. I honestly think he couldn't handle the thought of me feeling good about everything we've accomplished. For some sick reason, he isn't happy unless he pisses me off."

"Then he must've been downright ecstatic just now," Tristan said.

Nanette's green eyes widened in surprise, and then she laughed. "You know, I guess he was. I really shouldn't let him bait me like that. We got the answer we wanted, after all. The house is coming along okay, and as long as we don't have any new setbacks, particularly another hurricane, before we're done, we should be fine to finish—and to get funding from the historical society once they finish the restorations in Jefferson parish." She shook her head. "Everything's going fine, really."

"Glad to hear it," Tristan said, and then he watched as Nanette realized what she'd done.

"Have mercy, I just barged in here on you, didn't I? Chantelle, I'm sorry. I normally knock before I come in, but I wasn't thinking, and I really needed to talk to someone."

"You could've woken us up for the inspection," Tristan said. He'd actually planned on waking up early and helping her show the place to the committee, but after he and Chantelle had spent most of the night making love, he'd slept later than planned.

"I knew you were up late last night cleaning things up outside and didn't want to bother you," Nan said with a shrug.

Chantelle's leg nudged his, and Tristan knew she was probably thinking the same thing he was; they'd done a lot more outside than "clean up." He wondered if Nanette even realized that the two of them were naked beneath the sheets. Chantelle had the edges of the comforter tucked beneath her arms, and the covers were draped over his waist, but it wasn't all that difficult to see that they weren't clothed. However, maybe because her mind was on something else, or someone else—Charles Roussel, maybe?—Nanette didn't seem to notice and continued talking about the inspection.

"Besides, all I had to do was show them that the temporary supports were still doing the trick and that we were beginning to start on the repairs to that side. It wasn't hard. And Jenee was here for most of it, before she had to head to LSU for her first class." She squinted toward the clock on the bedside table, then frowned. "Hey, I've got to get to the school. I had to request a sub to watch my class until I arrived, but I'm supposed to give a test at ten. Are you off work today?" she asked Tristan.

"Yeah," he said. Even if he wasn't, he'd have requested time off so he could stay with Chantelle. There was no way he'd leave her for a long period until he was sure A. D. Romero was headed where he belonged. But if she was able to conquer her fear of being alone today, then that could very well happen before the day ended.

"Well, there's plenty of food in the kitchen—leftover gumbo and jambalaya in the fridge, and we still have plenty of boudin, too, if you want a sandwich."

"Thanks," Tristan said with a grin. He was nearly thirty, yet Nanette still found the need to mother him occasionally. He didn't mind, though, because it seemed to make her happy. At work, she mothered ninth graders; at home, she mothered anyone who happened to be around. Even now, with her thoughts on food for Tristan and Chantelle, her disposition had lightened considerably.

Then Nanette seemed to focus on the bed and the two of them in it, and she blushed, just a bit, but Tristan noticed. Took her long enough. "I...I'm leaving now," she said, backing out of the room and closing the door.

Chantelle waited a moment, then giggled. "I think she finally figured out we might have been in the middle of something."

"You think?" he asked, then indicated the covers at

his waist and the erection that was visible in spite of the layers on top of it.

She laughed again. "I asked you something right before she came in, you know."

He fell back against his pillow, draped his arm around her and pulled her on top of him. "Refresh my memory. What was the question again?"

She smirked and leaned over him, those long curls teasing his chest, neck and shoulders as she did, and her hot center teasing his cock even more. "I said I thought I needed an orgasm or two to get my day started right, before I tackle that last fear. And then I asked if you were going to give me what I need."

"Always."

Chantelle smiled her approval, then brought her soft mouth to his as she eased the tip of his penis into her wet opening.

Tristan focused on the kiss, enjoying the feel of her lips sliding across his, her tongue easing into his mouth, and did his best to put more of his attention on that than on the fact that her sweet center was ever so gradually easing down his length, holding him in her tight feminine folds.

Raw male instinct urged him to jerk his hips upward, thrust inside her with every ounce of power he possessed and fiercely claim her as his own. But that might hurt her, or scare her, and Tristan was intent on doing neither—ever. So he let her take this at her pace, guiding him deeper as her mouth left his and she began nuzzling his neck, then kissed his ear and nibbled at his lobe.

His guttural growl sounded like an animal in pain, but he couldn't help it; he was fighting his own body for control or, rather, forcing himself to hand over control to the woman he loved.

She nipped his lobe again, then whispered into his ear, her breath warm and her words incredibly erotic. "You need more, don't you?" she asked seductively. She finally allowed him entry completely, and Tristan tensed all over at the intoxicating pain of having her hold him there, so tightly, exactly where he wanted—but not giving him anything more. She didn't move, but those intimate walls were gently flexing around his cock, damn near breaking his will.

"This isn't enough for you, is it?" she repeated, and her voice was teasing him now, her smile evident in the words as she whispered them, hot and seductively, against his ear.

"No."

She rose above him, arching her hips to take his penis even deeper. She gave him a sultry smile as those golden curls tumbled wildly past her shoulders, teasing the tips of her full rose-tipped breasts and framing her nipples so they were even more prominently displayed.

"What do you want, Tristan? If this isn't enough, tell me what you want."

"Ride me. Ride me until you come."

She leaned forward again and kissed him deeply, thoroughly exploring the recesses of his mouth as her hips finally moved, her center sliding slowly up and down his length with an intoxicating rhythm. Not nearly fast enough, but enough to torture him, slowly, surely, and make him growl for more.

That growl caused her to break the kiss, and she braced her hands on his chest as the rhythm of her hips increased, and Tristan felt her growing hotter, wetter.

She slung her hair over one shoulder so she could peer at where the two of them joined, and she licked her lips as she watched. "Look at us," she whispered.

Tristan did, and damn near came from the sight. Evidently it had the same impact on Chantelle. She clutched his chest, her fingers inadvertently grabbing his nipples, causing his hips to jerk upward in instant response.

She noticed, and she didn't miss the opportunity to intensify this even more, pinching his nipples and ramming her hips down on him in direct correlation to his forceful thrusts. The slapping sound of skin to skin was almost as addictive as the near-pain of her fingers on his nipples, and Tristan gritted his teeth to hold on to the impending climax.

He reached between them and fiercely rubbed her clit with his thumb. Her muscles clenched even tighter around him and she threw her head back, gasping as she neared her release, then pumping him ferociously until finally, incredibly, their climaxes burst free.

"Tristan, Tristan!" She moved her hands from his chest to her own, gently rubbing her nipples as her undulating hips wound down slowly after the powerful release.

He'd thought she couldn't be more beautiful than when he brought her to orgasm, but he was wrong. Because there was something even more beautiful than Chantelle Bedeau losing control.

Chantelle Bedeau *in* control.

18

CHANTELLE STRETCHED in the bed and loved that her foot slid along Tristan's muscled leg as she did. The house was silent, the bedroom quiet, too, save for the steady sound of Tristan's breathing. She rolled onto her side and propped herself on her elbow to look at him, his tanned face and dark hair a striking contrast to the white pillow and sheet. He inhaled deeply, his chest expanding with the action, then he reached toward Chantelle and, feeling her beside him, hummed his contentment and drifted back to a sound sleep.

She smiled. This was such a wonderful way to spend the day, making love with Tristan until they fell asleep exhausted and sated, then sleeping enough to gain the energy to start over again. They'd started last night outside, then had continued through the night and after Nanette had left this morning, and Chantelle suspected that the two of them wouldn't stop there. They'd both need a shower whenever they actually got up, and after that bathing session two nights ago, she definitely wanted to experience shower sex, too.

She was still smiling when she eased away from the sleeping man in the bed and slipped into a T-shirt he'd left on the dresser. The clock beside the bed said that they'd slept past noon, and she knew Tristan was bound to be starving. *She* was. Plus, the brief interactions between him and Nanette each morning had given her an idea.

The stairs had yet to be replaced since Katrina's rising waters invaded the house, and some steps bowed upward while others dipped in the center. They creaked loudly as she descended, and she turned to verify that the eerie sound hadn't woken Tristan, though she'd closed the door to his room. She passed through the thick sheets of paint-splattered plastic closing off the majority of the first floor as she made her way to the kitchen. The lower rooms of the home had received the most damage from the storm, and Tristan and his family were still renovating them. It touched Chantelle's heart how determined they were in their efforts to save their home, the place that'd been so important to each of them when they grew up, and the place that was still important to them as adults, since the plantation house provided their sole means to communicate with spirits. Gage had received Lillian as an assignment in this home, and Chantelle would forever be grateful to him for helping her find the light, and for helping to stop A. D. Romero from killing anyone else.

She stepped into the kitchen and shivered, wishing that her thoughts of the Vicknairs' ghostly duties hadn't brought up memories of A.D. She tried to take her mind away from him by looking for filters for the coffee-maker perched on the counter near the sink. Twice Tristan had mentioned having coffee brought to him in bed, and Chantelle had tucked the information away for a time when she could surprise him by doing just that. It had been her goal when she started down to the kitchen, and now, she simply wanted to get the coffee made and take a cup to Tristan—without any additional thoughts of A. D. Romero and her past.

With her heart beating hard enough to feel it in her chest, she found a filter, filled the carafe with water and searched for the coffee. It wasn't in the freezer or the refrigerator, the places where she'd always kept it, so she assumed it was probably in one of the bulging black canisters on the opposite side of the sink. She opened each of them and found beans, rice and pasta. No coffee. Then she spotted a square wooden canister next to the knife block. "Coffee. Make the coffee and then get back to Tristan," she whispered to herself as she made her way toward the square canister. How would she conquer her fear of being by herself if she couldn't even come downstairs and make coffee without worrying that A.D. would make another appearance? Tristan didn't even have to leave the house for her to feel alone. She felt mighty isolated right now in this kitchen.

She unclasped the latch on the canister and was welcomed by the strong scent of coffee. "You're doing it now," she assured herself. "Being alone and facing the fear." She closed her eyes and inhaled the potent scent again, tried to let the familiar smell give her some form of comfort. But the hairs on the back of her neck prickled, and she dropped her hands to the counter. "Help me, Tristan," she said, and wished that he would hear her quivering voice and come down here to tell her everything would be okay. "What was I thinking?" she continued, and then gripped the countertop as nausea threatened to take control, her body queasy from the sudden change in temperature. The shock of painfully frigid air hitting her lungs made her gasp. "No!"

A loud bellowing echoed through the house. Tristan had shouted her name, and her eyes instinctively opened in time to see a knife rising from the block and moving toward her throat.

19

TRISTAN KNEW he was dreaming, but he didn't mind. The vision of Chantelle capturing his wrists and tying them to the headboard was so incredibly intoxicating that he didn't want it to end. Plus, when he awoke and when she'd had a chance to recover from their marathon of lovemaking throughout the night and morning, he'd describe this very scenario to her. Or perhaps he'd show her, tying her up first and bringing her to indescribable pleasure, and then letting her do the same to him.

He inhaled and smelled smoke, as strong and potent as any he'd ever encountered, and he coughed in his sleep. Though his eyes were closed, they still burned from the potency of the fire in his mind, and he heard the building roar of flames licking hungrily at wood.

"Hell," he muttered, knowing that the intensity of this feeling could only mean one thing. Another ghostly assignment was on the way or had already arrived on Grandma Adeline's tea service. Perhaps the arresting dream of Chantelle had kept him from noticing the obvious signs of a ghost's impending arrival, but now he couldn't avoid them. For one thing, he was covered in sweat and could practically feel the heat from the internal fire cooking his skin. Undoubtedly the realism of this particular ghost's calling card was stronger than usual due to his proximity to the sitting room down the hall. He really didn't want to deal with a ghost right now, or at least no ghost other than A. D. Romero, whom he hoped to send straight to hell before the day ended, when he and Chantelle conquered her final fear.

"I've got a ghost coming," he attempted to say, but was dismayed that his throat barely worked, the sensation of smoke invading his airway so real that it pained him to speak. And because of his attempt, he coughed more violently. This ghostly assignment was undeniably going to be one for the record books. Then he opened his eyes and realized the error of his assumptions. He wasn't coughing because a ghost was coming; he was coughing because he was surrounded by fire! And a ghost *was* here, but it wasn't one sent by Adeline Vicknair; it was A. D. Romero, back for Chantelle, who, Tristan realized with horror, was no longer in the bedroom.

"Chantelle!" he yelled, but he knew she couldn't hear him. How could she when the fire encompassing nearly half the room was at a deafening roar? Two walls, the one where the door was located and the one that led to the bathroom, were completely engulfed in vivid orange-and-yellow flames. He watched in horror as the red-and-silver can of accelerant that had been in the shed levitated in midair, then tilted to spill more of its golden liquid on the already billowing flames. The fire escalated immediately, roiling wildly toward the ceiling as the invisible ghost in Tristan's room fed it generously.

His firefighter instincts kicking in, Tristan quickly assessed his situation and formed a plan. Get out through the only viable exit, the window, and then get Chantelle—before A. D. Romero got to her. *If* he hadn't already. Tristan tried to climb off the bed, but found his hands tied firmly above his head. Hell, that part of his dream had been real, but it hadn't been Chantelle tying him up.

"Damn you, Romero!" He yanked at the ropes and only managed to pull them tighter.

More accelerant spilled toward the bed, and the flames eagerly followed. Tristan could almost hear the laughter of the ghost who was trying to burn him alive and murder Chantelle. Wasn't going to happen. No way in hell. Tristan edged up the bed and used his fingers to try to force slack into the knots around his wrists. Then, as the flames hit the comforter with a menacing *whoosh*, he used his teeth to pull at one edge of the outer loop of the knot—and smelled the putrid scent of hair burning. Still yanking at the knot with his teeth, he looked down to see the burning comforter near his left leg, close enough to singe the hair on his lower thigh. Tristan growled as he kicked the burning fabric away and blessedly felt the knot give.

With every bit of strength he possessed, he yanked his wrists free. Then, as the fire blazed across the sheets, he leaped off the bed and rolled to the window. Thank God, he'd thought to slip on his boxers during the night. Wouldn't that give someone a show? Before taking time to second-guess his decision—he had to find Chantelle—he opened the window and jumped.

CHANTELLE SCREAMED as the knife sped toward her throat, then she lunged backward, her hip connecting brutally with the kitchen table before she crumpled to the floor, the knife hitting the tile beside her noisily. Another knife scraped against the block as it was withdrawn powerfully, then moved backward in the air. She knew that A.D. held it and was about to throw it at her or stab her or…

Her mind reeled with possibilities—and with reality. The reality of coming face-to-face with her fear, the reality of A. D. Romero, her sister's murderer, attempting to kill her, as well, and the reality that the man she loved was upstairs, and she might very well never get to see him again, be with him again.

"No!" she screamed, flinging her body to the side as the second knife rushed toward her, this time at her chest. She didn't move quickly enough, and the blade sliced her shoulder and sent searing arrows of pain down her arm, through her side and up her throat. The knife, dripping with her blood, lifted again as A.D. prepared to stab her once more, and Chantelle's hatred for this man, for this ghost, pushed to the surface. "Damn you!"

The knife moved toward her, and Chantelle jerked to the side, then grabbed the handle and flung it away. "Damn you to hell! I *won't* let you take my life, and I *won't* let you take me away from Tristan! Damn you to hell!"

Her blood pumped fiercely, burning from the wound in her shoulder, but Chantelle didn't care.

At once, the kitchen was eerily silent and—thank God—the icy fear was gone.

Gone. Just like that.

The back door burst open and Tristan ran in, his body drenched with sweat and covered with bloody scratches and gouges. "Chantelle!" He rushed toward her, pulling her protectively into his arms, and then scanned the area surrounding her as though he might actually see A. D. Romero. "Where are you, you son of a bitch?"

"He's gone," she whispered as Gage and Kayla hurried into the kitchen.

"Are you two okay?" Gage asked.

"We're okay," Chantelle said, though her shoulder stung brutally. "Banged up, but okay."

"Damn," Tristan suddenly yelled. "The bedroom upstairs!"

"I saw." Gage grabbed a fire extinguisher from under the sink. "Kayla called 911. The fire department is on the way. Come on!"

Tristan suddenly saw Chantelle's shoulder, and the blood that now saturated the shirt she wore, *his* shirt. She'd put it on before starting downstairs to make coffee. Tristan turned, grabbed a towel near the sink and placed it over the wound. "Take her outside and hold this in place until the medics get here. I've got to help Gage," he told Kayla. Then he said to Chantelle, "You're sure you're okay?"

"Yes. Go help Gage."

"And you're sure he's gone?" Fire or no fire, Tristan was obviously not willing to leave her until he verified that A. D. Romero was no longer there.

"He's gone."

Tristan nodded and kissed her before running from the kitchen.

20

"YOU DON'T FEEL anything out of the ordinary?" Kayla asked, sitting in a porch rocker but leaning forward toward Chantelle. "You're sure he's gone?"

"I could tell the minute he left for good, the minute I'd conquered all my fears. I wasn't afraid anymore, and I wasn't going to let him win." Or take her away from the man she loved.

"Why do you think he set the place on fire?" Nanette asked. She was sitting in the rocker next to Kayla. Her voice was somewhat muffled because her hand was over her nose and mouth. The stench of the fire was still strong, even though it'd been out for hours, and they were all outside on the front porch of the house.

Chantelle shook her head. "I have no idea."

Tristan coughed, cleared his throat, then said, "I think he knew that he needed to keep me away from Chantelle in order for her fear to take control, and he somehow knew that I sense smoke and fire when I have a ghostly visit. Hell, there's no telling how long I stayed in bed thinking I was simply getting another assignment before I realized it was the real deal."

"I'm just glad Grandma Adeline's poinsettias are as stout and tall as they are," Nan declared. "Or you wouldn't have had anything to break your fall."

"Yeah, they broke the fall," Dax said. "But from the look of all of those scrapes and cuts on him, they didn't do it easily."

"They kept his bones from breaking, though," Celeste pointed out.

"Well, I'm glad we came back over here," Kayla said. "It scared me to death when we drove up and I saw Tristan jumping out of that window."

"Personally, *I'm* glad he had on boxers," Gage chimed in with a smirk, and they all laughed.

Chantelle scooted closer to Tristan, his arm protectively wrapped around her waist and away from the bandage that the medics had applied to the wound on her shoulder, which, thank God, wasn't deep. The knife had only slightly penetrated the flesh. She'd been amazed at how much blood had been produced, though, and she'd also been amazed at how badly the cut had burned. Then again, it may have hurt so intensely because of her fear, rather than the wound itself. But the fear had gone away, thanks to her determination not to let A. D. Romero succeed again—and to her determination not to leave Tristan.

"I'm sorry about the house," Chantelle said. "You've been trying so hard to get it fixed up, and because of me, you could've lost it." She thought of that bedroom, charred beyond recognition, and the fact that it would now also have heavy plastic sheets over its entrance like the rooms on the main floor. She'd come here for help, and they'd all willingly given it to her, and because of that, their house was worse for the wear. In this condition, there was no way the historical society would give them the funding they so desperately needed to restore it completely.

"Hey, the fire was contained to one room," Nanette reminded her. "And Tristan and all his men said that the smell won't last that long. Really, it's better that it happened right after the inspection, because now we have two months to get it all cleaned up before they see it. And you heard those guys from the firehouse— they're going to help us not only on weekends, but also on their days off."

"That's because of how well you feed them when they work," Tristan said, smiling. "Besides, the damage isn't all that bad compared to other places I've seen after fires."

"Yeah, and you saw Grandma Adeline's sitting room, didn't you? Nothing harmed there, and that's the only part of the house we need to worry about when it comes to the spirits," Gage added.

"I'm beginning to think that the entire house could burn down, and her room would remain intact. Neither fire, nor hurricane, nor an enraged ghost is going to mess with Grandma Adeline's sitting room." Monique grinned and rubbed her swollen belly as she spoke.

Ryan kissed her cheek. "Well, we all know how determined Vicknair women can be when they want something," he said, and she promptly elbowed him.

"But what *are* you going to do about that bedroom?" Chantelle asked, still feeling a bit guilty about her part in the fire. She really couldn't fathom how they'd get the house up to the committee's standards in two months, even with the extra help.

"Like Nan said, the firefighters will devote all their spare time to working on our place," Tristan said. "And my men are nothing if not determined, but I'm sure they'd appreciate it next time if you didn't come driving up trying to hit ninety in your Beetle while they're trying to work."

"Won't happen again," she promised, and began to believe that maybe with the help of his firehouse crew and all the family chipping in, that room could be salvaged, and she would no longer feel as though she'd ruined their chances at saving their home from demolition. And she could help financially. "You know, I'll be pitching my next book to my editor soon. I should have a decent advance, enough to help with repair costs to that room."

"You don't have to do that," Nanette said.

"I want to. Besides, I owe my novel's premise to the Vicknair plantation house. It's only right for some of the proceeds to keep it standing."

Nanette grinned. "In that case, okay. *Some* proceeds, but not all." She paused. "I didn't ever ask you what made the two of you come back," she said to Gage. "I thought you had to work at the hospital today." And then to Kayla she said, "And I thought you were scheduled to meet with someone about reopening the orphanage. Or do I have my dates wrong?"

"No, you're right," Gage said, moving to the rocker on the other side of Kayla and taking her hand in his as he spoke. "But with everything going on, Kayla moved her meeting to early this morning, and I swapped shifts with one of the other doctors so I could have the rest of the day off, after Kayla gave me the news."

"What news?"

"Go on," Gage told Kayla.

Her smile claimed her entire face. "We wanted to be here when you got home from work so we could tell you," she said to Nanette. "And we called Ryan, Monique, Dax and Celeste to come over, as well. I guess it was lucky that we did, since everyone got here in time to help put the fire out."

Dax and Celeste were sitting on the top porch step, and they turned to listen. "Well, we're all here, so what news are we talking about?" Dax asked, snuggling Celeste as he spoke.

"First, with Rosa and Jenee's help, we got the approval from the state to reopen the Seven Sisters."

Chantelle's chest tightened automatically when Kayla said the name of the orphanage where she, Kayla, Lillian and Shelby had spent a large portion of their youth—and where they'd been abused by A.D. and Wayne Romero. Kayla was determined to turn the place into something good, the type of loving environment Rosa had envisioned when she and her mother opened the home so long ago. Chantelle was truly glad that the orphanage was going to end up being someplace positive, and she had no doubt that if anyone could pull it off, it would be Kayla, Jenee and Rosa.

"It's going to be a refuge for girls who've been abused, primarily teens, but probably a few young women, too."

"That's wonderful," Chantelle said, emotion causing her voice to crack as she spoke, and Tristan squeezed her waist reassuringly. "I'll help any way I can."

"Thank you," Kayla said, still smiling. "And then, there's the biggest news…"

Chantelle knew what news this would be. Kayla had obviously taken the pregnancy test and received confirmation she was going to have Gage's child.

Chantelle thought of Wayne Romero's trial and what they'd all gone through by that time, and how each of them had wondered if they'd ever have normal lives. It'd been so difficult getting over the past, but Shelby was now happily married to Phillip, Kayla was madly in love with Gage and had a new baby on the way, and Chantelle had found the man of her dreams. Tears pressed forward, and she wiped them away. She only wished Lillian were still here to see Kayla make her announcement—and to know that Chantelle had finally found peace, as well.

Something soft touched her cheek, and Chantelle moved her hand from wiping her tears to that very spot—where she knew Lillian had just kissed her. Lillian *was* here; she was watching, as Chantelle knew she often did, and she was happy for them. Her heart swelled. Life was good, better than good. It was almost perfect.

Kayla completed her announcement and the family promptly cheered. Kayla and Gage accepted hugs and congratulations from all around, and then Gage scanned the group and realized it was missing one Vicknair. "Where's Jenee?"

"Oh, as soon as our meeting ended this morning, she said she had to tend to her ghost," Kayla answered.

"She got an assignment?" Nanette asked, shocked. "I knew she'd been sleeping a lot lately and that she said one was coming, but she didn't say anything about a letter arriving. Does she need help with her ghost?"

"I don't think a letter has come," Kayla said. "But she kept saying that he was pulling at her and causing her to need more sleep."

"Sounds like this one is having a hard time even finding his way to the middle so he can *get* help," Celeste joked. She knew what that was like, since she'd spent quite a bit of time in the middle realm while in a coma before finding her way back to Dax.

"I guess." Kayla shrugged. "But in any case, she decided to stay at Rosa's place and go back to bed so he could communicate with her again."

"Seems like she'd have come here, so she'd be near the sitting room when her assignment comes," Nanette said.

"Well, she should've." Gage grinned. "Because then she'd have been here to hear the news."

"I'll tell her later today," Kayla offered. "I'm assuming it'll mean that she has to take a bigger part in getting the Seven Sisters up and running over the next few months, with me having morning sickness and all."

"Oh, it's really something, isn't it?" Monique commiserated, and she and Kayla began exchanging pregnancy stories and discussing the types of foods Monique had found to have staying power in her stomach.

Chantelle looked at Tristan, his attention riveted on the two pregnant women in the family, and she wondered what he'd look like one day when he learned that he was going to have a child. And then she wondered what it'd feel like one day to tell him that news. But first, she needed to tell him something equally important. "Can we talk in private?" she whispered.

He nodded, and then the two of them discreetly left the other Vicknairs chatting about babies. "The cane field or the levee?" he asked, identifying the two most private places around.

"Levee," she said, and the two walked the magnolia-lined driveway in contented silence as they made their way across River Road and up the bank. The cane reeds growing on the levee's edge whistled from the breeze blowing off the Mississippi, and large flat barges pushed noisily through the churning brown water.

"You okay?" he asked after they'd taken a moment to survey the uniqueness of their surroundings. The combination of River Road, the levee and the Mississippi formed a mesmerizing display, as exceptional as the family that lived across the road, and as the man standing beside her now. "You aren't feeling him anymore, are you?" Tristan continued, and she shook her head.

"No," she said, looking at him, at the way the breeze teased his dark hair, the way his green eyes captured the last light of day and shone with intensity. He *was* intense, thrilling and compelling. And he was the man she wanted more than anything else, the one who'd saved her life. When she could have let A. D. Romero have control in that kitchen, she hadn't, because her thoughts had been of surviving—with Tristan.

"No," she repeated. "I don't feel him at all, and I'm sure he's now gone where he was supposed to go. But I did need to tell you something else, about everything."

"Okay," he said. "Tell me, Chantelle. What is it?"

"I didn't list all my fears that day, because there was one that I couldn't admit, not aloud, and particularly not to you. But I've faced that one, too, and I know now that it was as important for me to conquer that one as any other, and I did."

His dark brows edged upward. "What fear?"

Chantelle looked out at the water, the way it seemed

to churn even harder around those barges, as though determined to make them go in the direction it wanted them to go. It would've been much easier for those ships to give up, to surrender to the sheer power of the mighty river's pull. But they didn't. And it would've been much easier for her to give up, as well, to surrender to her horrid destiny and never experience everything a woman should, never have a real relationship—and never conquer that final fear.

"I was afraid...of falling in love." She eased toward him, so close that she felt the heat of him against her, and she loved the way it felt, being nearly one with him. "I'd lost everyone I ever truly loved—my parents, Lillian—and I didn't know if I could let my heart risk the possibility of losing someone else. Then, when I thought A.D. was going to take me away from you, I realized that love, true love, is worth the risk. And I realized how much I love you, Tristan. I'm deeply, madly, wonderfully in love with you."

"Chantelle, I—"

A car horn blasting from the road nearby halted his proclamation, and they both turned to see Jenee, her hand waving out her car window as she pulled into the driveway of the plantation house across the street.

Tristan grinned. "Good. I'm glad my sister will be there for this."

"For this?"

"We'll wait a few minutes, give Kayla and Gage enough time to make their announcements again in front of Jenee, but then, we'll need to let them know that there's more good news to go around."

Chantelle could feel her pulse increasing with anxious anticipation. "More good news?"

"I love you, too, Chantelle," he said. "And I don't plan to spend another day of my life without you by my side. So, if you'll say yes, I'm thinking the two of us can make this one of the best days in Vicknair history. A baby on the way for Gage and Kayla, and another wedding to plan—for us. Will you marry me, Chantelle Bedeau?"

"Yes."

Tristan placed the most gentle kiss on Chantelle's lips, and she shivered, but this wasn't the kind of shiver she'd experienced whenever A. D. Romero was near; this wasn't sheer terror. It was sheer…perfection.

* * * * *

Which medium will be the next to experience
a ghostly encounter of the most sensual kind?
Don't miss BED ON ARRIVAL available July 2008

THOROUGHBRED LEGACY
*The stakes are high when it comes to love,
horse racing, family secrets
and broken promises.*

*A new exciting Harlequin continuity series
coming soon!*
Led by New York Times *bestselling author
Elizabeth Bevarly*
FLIRTING WITH TROUBLE

Here's a preview!

THE DOOR CLOSED behind them, throwing them into darkness and leaving them utterly alone. And the next thing Daniel knew, he heard himself saying, "Marnie, I'm sorry about the way things turned out in Del Mar."

She said nothing at first, only strode across the room and stared out the window beside him. Although he couldn't see her well in the darkness—he still hadn't switched on a light…but then, neither had she—he imagined her expression was a little preoccupied, a little anxious, a little confused.

Finally, very softly, she said, "Are you?"

He nodded, then, worried she wouldn't be able to see the gesture, added, "Yeah. I am. I should have said goodbye to you."

"Yes, you should have."

Actually, he thought, there were a lot of things he should have done in Del Mar. He'd had *a lot* riding on the Pacific Classic, and even more on his entry, Little Joe, but after meeting Marnie, the Pacific Classic had been the last thing on Daniel's mind. His loss at Del Mar had pretty much ended his career before it had even begun, and he'd had to start all over again, rebuilding from nothing.

He simply had not then and did not now have room in his life for a woman as potent as Marnie Roberts. He was a horseman first and foremost. From the time he was a schoolboy, he'd known what he wanted to do with his life—be the best possible trainer he could be.

He had to make sure Marnie understood—and he understood, too—why things had ended the way they had eight years ago. He just wished he could find the words to do that. Hell, he wished he could find the *thoughts* to do that.

"You made me forget things, Marnie, things that I really needed to remember. And that scared the hell out of me. Little Joe should have won the Classic. He was by far the best horse entered in that race. But I didn't give him the attention he needed and deserved that week, because all I could think about was you. Hell, when I woke up that morning all I wanted to do was lie there and look at you, and then wake you up and make love to you again. If I hadn't left when I did—the way I did—I might still be lying there in that bed with you, thinking about nothing else."

"And would that be so terrible?" she asked.

"Of course not," he told her. "But that wasn't why I was in Del Mar," he repeated. "I was in Del Mar to win a race. That was my job. And my work was the most important thing to me."

She said nothing for a moment, only studied his face in the darkness as if looking for the answer to a very important question. Finally she asked, "And what's the most important thing to you now, Daniel?"

Wasn't the answer to that obvious? "My work," he answered automatically.

She nodded slowly. "Of course," she said softly. "That is, after all, what you do best."

Her comment, too, puzzled him. She made it sound as if being good at what he did was a bad thing.

She bit her lip thoughtfully, her eyes fixed on his, glimmering in the scant moonlight that was filtering through the window. And damned if Daniel didn't find himself wanting to pull her into his arms and kiss her. But as much as it might have felt as if no time had passed since Del Mar, there were eight years between now and then. And eight years was a long time in the best of circumstances. For Daniel and Marnie, it was virtually a lifetime.

So Daniel turned and started for the door, then halted. He couldn't just walk away and leave things as they were, unsettled. He'd done that eight years ago and regretted it.

"It *was* good to see you again, Marnie," he said softly. And since he was being honest, he added, "I hope we see each other again."

She didn't say anything in response, only stood silhouetted against the window with her arms wrapped around her in a way that made him wonder whether she was doing it because she was cold, or if she just needed something—someone—to hold on to. In either case, Daniel understood. There was an emptiness clinging to him that he suspected would be there for a long time.

* * * * *

THOROUGHBRED LEGACY
coming soon wherever books are sold!

Thoroughbred Legacy

Launching in June 2008

A dramatic new 12-book continuity that embodies the American Dream.

Meet the Prestons, owners of Quest Stables, a successful horse-racing and breeding empire. But the lives, loves and reputations of this hardworking family are put at risk when a breeding scandal unfolds.

Flirting with Trouble

by *New York Times* bestselling author

ELIZABETH BEVARLY

Eight years ago, publicist Marnie Roberts spent seven days of bliss with Australian horse trainer Daniel Whittleson. But just as quickly, he disappeared. Now Marnie is heading to Australia to finally confront the man she's never been able to forget.

The stakes are high when it comes to love, horse racing, family secrets and broken promises.

A new exciting Harlequin continuity series coming soon!

www.eHarlequin.com

Silhouette Desire

Cole's Red-Hot Pursuit

Cole Westmoreland is a man who gets what he wants. And he wants independent and sultry Patrina Forman! She resists him—until a Montana blizzard traps them together. For three delicious nights, Cole indulges Patrina with his brand of seduction. When the sun comes out, Cole and Patrina are left to wonder—will this be the end of the passion that storms between them?

Look for

COLE'S RED-HOT PURSUIT

by USA TODAY bestselling author

BRENDA JACKSON

Available in June 2008 wherever you buy books.

Always Powerful, Passionate and Provocative.

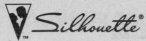

Romantic
SUSPENSE

Sparked by Danger,
Fueled by Passion.

Seduction Summer:
Seduction in the sand...and a killer on the beach.

Silhouette Romantic Suspense invites you to the hottest summer yet with three connected stories from some of our steamiest storytellers! Get ready for...

Killer Temptation
by Nina Bruhns;
a millionaire this tempting is worth a little danger.

Killer Passion
by Sheri WhiteFeather;
an FBI profiler's forbidden passion incites a
killer's rage,

and

Killer Affair
by Cindy Dees;
this affair with a mystery man is to die for.

Look for

KILLER TEMPTATION by Nina Bruhns in June 2008
KILLER PASSION by Sheri WhiteFeather in July 2008
and
KILLER AFFAIR by Cindy Dees in August 2008.

Available wherever you buy books!

Visit Silhouette Books at www.eHarlequin.com   SRS27586

REQUEST YOUR FREE BOOKS!

2 FREE NOVELS PLUS 2 FREE GIFTS!

HARLEQUIN®

Blaze™

Red-hot reads!

HB08

Royal Seductions

Michelle Celmer delivers a powerful miniseries in
Royal Seductions, where two brothers fight for the
crown and discover love. In *The King's Convenient Bride*,
the king discovers his marriage of convenience to the
woman he's been promised to wed is turning all too
real. The playboy prince proposes a mock engagement
to defuse rumors circulating about him and restore
order to the kingdom...until his pretend fiancée
becomes pregnant in *The Illegitimate Prince's Baby*.

Look for

THE KING'S CONVENIENT BRIDE
&
THE ILLEGITIMATE PRINCE'S BABY

BY MICHELLE CELMER

Available in June 2008 wherever you buy books.

Always Powerful, Passionate and Provocative.

HARLEQUIN®
Blaze™

COMING NEXT MONTH

#399 CROSSING THE LINE Lori Wilde
Perfect Anatomy
Confidential Rejuvenations, an exclusive Texas boutique clinic, has a villain on the loose. But it's the new surgeon, Dr. Dante Nash, who is getting the most attention from chief nurse Elle Kingston....

#400 THE LONER Rhonda Nelson
Men Out of Uniform
Lucas "Huck" Finn is thrilled to join Ranger Security—until he learns his new job is to babysit Sapphira Stravos, a doggie-toting debutante. Still, he knows there's more to Sapphira than meets the eye. And what's meeting the eye is damn hard to resist.

#401 NOBODY DOES IT BETTER Jennifer LaBrecque
Lust in Translation
Gage Carswell, British spy, is all about getting his man—or in this case, his woman. He's after Holly Smith, whom he believes to be a notorious agent. And he's willing to do anything—squire her around Venice, play out all her sexual fantasies—to achieve his goal. Too bad this time *his* woman isn't the *right* woman.

#402 SLOW HANDS Leslie Kelly
The Wrong Bed: Again and Again
Heiress Madeleine Turner only wants to stop her stepmother from making a huge mistake. That's how she ends up buying Jake Wallace at a charity bachelor auction. But now that she's won the sexy guy, what's she going to do with him? Lucky for her, Jake has a few ideas....

#403 SEX BY THE NUMBERS Marie Donovan
Blush
Accountant—undercover! Pretending to be seriously sexy Dane Weiss's ditsy personal assistant to secretly hunt for missing company funds isn't what Keeley Davis signed up for. But the overtime is out of this world!

#404 BELOW THE BELT Sarah Mayberry
Jamie Sawyer wants to redeem her family name in the boxing world. To do that, she needs trainer Cooper Fitzgerald. Spending time together ignites a sizzling attraction...one he's resisting. Looks as if she'll have to aim her best shots a little low to get what she wants.

HBCNM0508